"You're Still A Rowdy Cowboy, Aren't You?"

Kelly said, her eyes dropping to his lips. "This isn't the place for lovemaking."

"Honey, anywhere I want is the place." Kit slipped his hand up beneath her hair, encircling her neck. Drawing her near, his mouth closed over hers in a hungry kiss. His lips pressed against hers, moving persuasively until she parted her own and felt the gentle entry of his tongue. She forgot the dance, the townspeople and their charade as she reveled in the sweet sensations rippling through her at his touch.

She was breathing erratically when he released her. "Is that called staking your claim?" she asked, her voice tremulous.

"Yep." His eyes roamed the room in blatant satisfaction before he looked back at her. "And everyone who needed to know it, saw."

Dear Reader,

When *Man of the Month* began back in 1989, no one knew it would become the reader favorite it is today. Sure, we thought we were on to a good thing. After all, one of the reasons we read romance is for the great heroes! But the program was a *phenomenal* success, and now, over six years later, we are celebrating our 75th *Man of the Month*—and that's something to be proud of.

The very first *Man of the Month* was *Reluctant Father* by Diana Palmer. So who better to write the 75th *Man of the Month* than this wonderful author? In addition, this terrific story, *That Burke Man,* is also part of her LONG, TALL TEXANS series—so it's doubly special.

There are also five more great Desire books this month: *Accidental Bride* by Jackie Merritt; *One Stubborn Cowboy* by Barbara McMahon; *The Pauper and the Pregnant Princess* by Nancy Martin—which begins her OPPOSITES ATTRACT series; *Bedazzled* by Rita Rainville; and *Texas Heat* by Barbara McCauley— which begins her HEARTS OF STONE series.

This March, Desire is certainly the place to be. Enjoy!

Lucia Macro,
Senior Editor

Please address questions and book requests to:
Silhouette Reader Service
U.S.: 3010 Walden Ave., P.O. Box 1325, Buffalo, NY 14269
Canadian: P.O. Box 609, Fort Erie, Ont. L2A 5X3

BARBARA McMAHON
ONE STUBBORN COWBOY

SILHOUETTE *Desire*®
Published by Silhouette Books
America's Publisher of Contemporary Romance

SILHOUETTE BOOKS

ISBN 0-373-05915-9

ONE STUBBORN COWBOY

BARBARA McMAHON

was born and raised in the South. She traveled around the world while working for an international airline, then settled down to raise a family and work for a computer firm. She began writing when her children started school. Now that she has been fortunate enough to realize her long-held dream of quitting her "day job" and writing full-time, she and her husband have moved from the San Francisco Bay area to the Sierra Nevada mountains of California. With the beauty of the mountains visible from her windows, and the pace of life slower, she finds more time than ever to think up stories and share them with others. Barbara also writes for Harlequin Romance.

Kelly-Anne, this one's for you!

One

There was no warning.

One minute Kelly was calmly crossing the deserted country road heading for the feed and grain. The next moment a large pickup truck tore out of the barnlike building, its tires squealing on the pavement as it skidded in the turn. Righting itself, it headed directly for Kelly.

Jumping out of the way at the last second, she felt surprise and fear clash within her, producing instant anger. Kelly caught her breath and turned after the truck. "Dammit, you imbecile! Watch where you're going! Do you think you own the blasted road?" Her heart was pounding at the near miss. She could have been killed!

The truck slammed on its brakes and began backing up.

After twenty-eight years in San Francisco with nary an accident, she couldn't believe she had almost been run down by the only moving vehicle on an otherwise deserted road. She was furious. Just who did that driver think he was to come barreling out of the building like that? There could have been children crossing the road, or an elderly person who wouldn't have moved as quickly as she had.

"Just you wait," Kelly murmured between clenched teeth as she watched the truck draw closer.

The pickup truck was white-and-blue with big all-terrain tires, the jacked-up body and the mud splatters along the sides giving evidence of its off-road travels. It backed up quickly, drawing to a stop beside her.

Kelly held her ground until the cab of the truck was even with her, the throaty growl of its engine loud in the afternoon stillness. She'd often been teased she should have red hair instead of blond, to match her temper. It boiled over now. She'd give this reckless driver a piece of her mind. Maybe next time he wouldn't be so quick to drive so wildly.·

The truck was higher than usual. She had to look up to see into the darker interior. As the driver glared back down at her, she drew a breath in shock. If she had thought she was angry, it was nothing compared to the visage of the man facing her. Narrowed black eyes looked out at her from under a jutting brow creased in an angry frown. His eyebrows almost met, his frown was so ferocious. His lips were thinned, tight with hostility. She could feel the strength of his emotions almost envelop her.

"What the hell did you call me?" He was a big man, with wide, strong shoulders, muscular arms, strong, chiseled features. His expression was grim, his voice harsh and deep.

Kelly's emotions flared, her blood boiling. He had a hell of a nerve being mad.

"I called you an imbecile. Idiot might apply, as well. Who do you think you are, pulling out like that? What if someone who couldn't move fast had been crossing the street? This is California—didn't you know pedestrians have the right of way?" she said, her teeth still gritted. She tilted her chin defiantly, her own blue eyes blazing with anger. "You could have killed me with your reckless driving! Do you think you own the damn road?" Her glare was like ice, challenging his, never wavering.

"What did you call me?" he growled again between clenched teeth, his gaze raking her as she stood defiantly in the hot sun. His eyes moved insolently from her flushed, angry face to her breasts, heaving with emotion. Pausing only a moment, they drifted lower, to her trim waist, flaring hips and long legs encased in stone-washed jeans.

Kelly felt a frisson of a different kind of anger run through her. How dare this man look at her like that, as if she was on exhibit! She held her ground resolutely, feeling the heat of her indignation build.

"I called you an *imbecile*. You hard of hearing? You drive like a maniac, accelerating out of there like that, without seeing if anyone was in the street. Where'd you get your license, out of a cereal box?" she asked scornfully. For a split second Kelly wondered what she'd do if he got out of the truck. He was so big, and looked mean.

"You're new around here, aren't you?" he said softly, the change menacing. "So I'll give you some advice. Don't *ever* talk to me again like that, or you'll be sorry!" His hands were tight on the steering wheel, his face shadowed by his hat.

Kelly shivered in spite of the hot day. She could feel his resolve as he said the words. But she had grown up in some tough neighborhoods. She wasn't easily intimidated, certainly not by some reckless cowboy in the wrong. She continued staring at him, tilting her chin defiantly.

"Oh, yeah? What are you gonna do about it?" she flung back. Just let him open the door and try something. She knew a move or two that might surprise him. Self-defense was a way of life, a part of growing up in the city, and she'd studied different ways to keep safe.

His lips tightened, then he let his eyes wander again insolently down the length of her, his expression changing.

"Sure of yourself, aren't you?" Was there a trace of amusement in his tone?

Kelly felt the wave of hot color wash over her. She wished he *would* get out of the truck. Her hand clenched in a tight fist. She'd like to wipe that insolent look off his face, show him she wasn't to be intimidated by some small-town, hot-shot, cocky cowboy.

Before she could reply, however, the old owner of B.J.'s Feed and Grain came around the back of the truck, slapping his hand hard against the metal side.

"What's going on out here?" Jefferies asked, the wizened man peering between Kelly and the driver.

"Just welcoming a newcomer," the man drawled mockingly, raising one eyebrow as if daring Kelly to challenge his audacious statement.

Her angry gaze never left his face. His straw cowboy hat was pulled low on his forehead, throwing his face in shadow. She could make out his eyes now, despite the low brim. They were not black as she'd first thought, but a dark, stormy blue. Dark brown hair hung beneath his hat, brushing the collar of his checked shirt. It was thick and springy. She wished for a second she could see him without the hat. Wished he would get down from the truck and face off. Her heart began to beat faster in anticipation.

"You go on home, Kit. Kelly has the right of it. Next time don't pull out so fast if you can't see that the way's clear!" the old man admonished.

With a quick glance at Jefferies the driver seemed to calm down. His gaze returned to Kelly and he gave her another mocking look. "We'll have to continue this interesting discussion at another time." The man put the truck in gear and accelerated, tires squealing on the blacktop as he pulled away.

Kelly watched the truck speed down the highway, the air still charged from their encounter, her heart racing. Had he looked this time before pulling away? Probably not. Who was he? She'd not met him before. Kelly would never have forgotten him. Would he be back soon?

She turned to Jefferies, a smile settling on her face. "Thanks for coming out. I thought for a minute he was going to get out and knock me down." Had she hoped he would try? She would have liked to see him. Was he as tall as he looked sitting in the cab of the truck?

"Not to worry." Spying her sketch pad and pencils his face lightened. "You've come to draw the old place? Molly said you were an artist."

She smiled and nodded, casting another quick glance at the departing truck. "That and a writer. I illustrate my own books. I thought to sketch the feed store, if that's all right with you."

"Come on in, then. Don't you go worrying about yon Kit—he's hotheaded and wild, but he doesn't come to town much anymore. He knows he was in the wrong, though it didn't make him happy, did it?" Jefferies chuckled. "Sure was fun, watching you stand up to him. Not many people do, poor boy." Jefferies shook his head as they walked into the dim feed store.

Kelly could see no reason for Jefferies to consider that insufferable, arrogant man poor, or a boy. From the weathered look of his face he must be well into his thirties. And what he probably needed was more people to stand up to him. Who was he anyway, the town bully?

She could tell him a thing or two. As always after an emotionally charged event, Kelly thought up several scathing comments she should have made. She glanced down the street once more, wishing she'd had a little longer to tell him off. Wondering when she'd see him again.

It took Kelly a few minutes to calm down and capture the mood she needed to sketch pictures. Over and over her mind replayed the truck roaring toward her, the angry man driving it. Each time her heart sped up with the memory. It had been unexpected and frightening. Yet the driver had intrigued her.

His chin had been strong and firm with deep lines carving his cheeks, bracketing his mouth. His skin had been dark and tanned like a rancher or cowboy. But the dark blue eyes were unexpected, especially with his dark hair. His shoulders and height indicated a tall, large man. She remembered his muscular arms, the strong hands on the wheel. Was he a cowboy or a rancher? Did he live near town, come in often? Jefferies had said not. Who was he?

With an effort she dragged her thoughts back to the sketches she wanted to do. Soothed by the deft strokes of her pencils, she settled in to draw different scenes of the unusual store from a child's point of view, trying to capture the aspects that would appeal to children. The drawings began to take shape. But at the back of her mind was the question of who Kit was. And when she might see him again.

Kit Lockford drove his pickup at a breakneck speed. But his mind was not on his driving—he was wondering who the woman was. He'd never seen her before, didn't have a clue to who she was or why she was in town. But Jefferies obviously knew her. Was she visiting, or had she recently moved in?

He grinned, remembering how she'd yelled at him. No brains probably, like most blondes. And a pretty blonde at that with her long, white-blond hair and big, sky blue eyes. Her figure wasn't bad, either. He chuckled at the dumb-blonde stereotype, not believing it for a moment, but he bet it would make her mad as hell to hear him say it.

He tried to recall if he'd seen a ring on her left hand. She had been holding some sort of pad, but he didn't think she had a ring. For a moment he thought about turning around and heading back for B.J.'s Feed and Grain, and seeing if she was still there. See if she'd light into him again with her complaints about his driving.

She sure had guts, he thought, thinking about her temper with another grin. He was a big man, had a bad temper himself. Yet she'd yelled at him as no one had in years. His grin faded. And she'd probably never do it again. He hated the way everyone tried to coddle him, to tiptoe around him. Once she found out about him, she'd be like the rest. Damn!

Turning in to the driveway that led home some time later, he turned his thoughts elsewhere. No use thinking of the woman. They'd probably never meet again. Or if they did, it would be after she knew all about Kit Lockford, and her attitude would be different. He wished he could see her once more before she knew. He'd hate to see pity from her eyes. But it would be too much to hope he'd escape it.

"You stay away from young Kit Lockford," Molly Benson admonished Kelly later that afternoon.

Kelly looked up at her next-door neighbor in surprise, her eyes dancing in amusement. "How did you know I met him?" He now had a last name. Lockford.

The two were sipping iced tea, beneath the large oak tree that straddled their property lines. Kelly had visited with the old woman almost every day since she had arrived in Taylorville five days ago. Molly Benson was in her eighties. She'd been a friend of Kelly's great-aunt, and Kelly wanted to learn as much about her as she could. Molly had endless stories to tell.

"Small town, news travels fast," Molly said gently.

"We weren't actually introduced." Kelly smiled in remembrance, the incident almost amusing in retrospect, now that she could forget how frightened she'd been. Actually, she was having trouble not thinking about the cowboy.

"You probably won't be introduced any time soon. He and his brother own one of the big ranches outside town. Raise cattle, naturally. Kit doesn't come in much anymore. How Clint puts up with him, I just don't know." Molly shook her head, gazing across her yard toward the grassy hills in the distance.

"A hellion, huh?" Kelly asked, remembering what Jefferies had said. She was curious about the man, and wondered what Molly would tell her.

"He was always chasing wild times and wild women. I didn't think he'd ever settle down. He was hotheaded and stubborn, thought he was God's gift to the ladies and wanted to pleasure as many as he could when he was younger."

Kelly hid a smile and glanced away. How odd to hear that from Molly. She seemed too much an old-fashioned lady to even know about wild young men and their pleasures, much less mention it in public.

"But he doesn't come to town much anymore?" Kelly asked. How could she learn more without Molly suspecting her interest? Kelly was oddly shy about showing overt interest in the man. Though her curiosity was raging.

"No. Good thing, I tell you. At least the girls are safe again."

Kelly couldn't help smiling broadly at that. She'd only seen the man for a few moments, but she could understand how some women would be drawn to him. He was raw masculinity personified. Even angry, he'd stopped and looked at her, really looked at her, and made her feel every inch a woman. For a few seconds she let herself imagine what it would be like to have him look at her when he wasn't angry. She wasn't prepared for the surge of desire and anticipation that swept through her at the thought. It shook her.

No use thinking in those terms. She'd be way out of her depth with that man. She was used to the conservative businessmen and gentle artists she knew from San Francisco. Not an earthy, brash, wild cowboy looking to pleasure any woman around.

Fixing dinner that night, Kelly was pleased when she realized how satisfied she was with her new lifestyle. It had been an experiment, coming to Taylorville. Yet it seemed destined, somehow. When she had first learned of her inheritance, the large old house in the heart of a small ranching community, she'd been shocked. She had not known she had a great-aunt and had never expected an inheritance. She had always thought of herself as alone. Orphaned when young, she had not known she had any living relatives. It had been kind of her unknown aunt to leave her the house, but she wished she had tried to contact her while she'd lived.

She smiled wryly as she set the table, remembering how her friends had taken the news of her move. Maybe she was crazy as they'd said. But she was tired of traffic jams, rude street people and the growing crime rate in San Francisco.

She wanted to try a change of life-style. And being a writer, she could work anywhere, so why not move?

But her friends greeted her news with incredulity, disbelief, flat-out denial. Her agent thought she'd lost her mind; her friend Susan suspected a man was involved; and her neighbor David refused to believe she was serious, even when he helped her pack her car.

"You'll be back in a week," he'd said in continued disbelief. "If you last that long."

Kelly only smiled. They'd been friends for years, and knew each other well. He could be right, though she wasn't planning on it. She wanted to make the change. Now the first week was drawing to a close and she wasn't ready to leave yet. The experiment had just begun, and she liked it!

Looking back over the five days, Kelly was astonished at how easily she'd transplanted. Reared in various neighborhoods of San Francisco, her only previous experience with the country had been forays into Golden Gate Park, and one long weekend in Yosemite. Yet she found the quiet, slow pace of life easy to adjust to, and in only a few days she felt as if she'd always had a place in Taylorville, as if she belonged. And that was a wonderful feeling, one she'd been looking for all her life. To belong.

The next morning Kelly studied her sketches, deciding which she would paint. Her charcoal renditions of the feed store were good. Just needed a touch here and there. She was still trying to formulate a story line that would use the store. Without meaning to, she began to think about her encounter yesterday.

Startled, she realized she was sketching Kit Lockford. She started to rip out the page, hesitated, then changed her mind. Concentrating on his image, she quickly added bold strokes to the picture. The likeness was perfect. She'd done a good job capturing his hostility, and the hidden but discernible aching hurt.

She paused and stared at the picture in disbelief. Why in the world would she think there was hurt reflected in those bold, stormy eyes? A more self-confident, arrogant, *irritating* man she had yet to meet. He acted as if he owned the whole damn town. Or at least the road that ran through it. And his look when he'd surveyed her had definitely been insolent male appraisal.

Flipping over her page, she began another picture. She wouldn't think about Kit Lockford again. Blast the man, she'd only talked to him for about four minutes—why couldn't she forget the incident? Forget the way he looked, forget the way she tensed up inside whenever she remembered how he'd raked her with his gaze.

She sketched a small black pony, dozing alone in a field. She'd seen the pony on one of her driving explorations around the county and had immediately wanted a story centered around him. But she didn't like the sketch. Tearing it up, she tried again. It just wasn't right. Somehow she wasn't getting the proper perspective. Frustrated, Kelly stood, stretched and went to her window. She needed to see some horses in action. Her pony was too stiff, too artificial.

Her eyes lit up. There were ranches all around. Surely she could visit one and study their horses, watch how they moved, capture the action on paper.

As she turned, the thought flashed in her mind that Kit Lockford had a ranch. Of course he'd have horses on it—it was a working cattle ranch according to Molly. Not that she'd go to his ranch. She'd ask around town for someone to recommend a ranch. If they recommended the Lockford place, maybe she'd go. A bubble of excitement grew as she considered visiting his ranch. Would he let her sketch his horses? Or would he still be angry at her for calling him an idiot and refuse? Well, there were other ranches.

Buoyed by her plan, Kelly dressed in jeans and a cool cotton top, smiling as she did so. It felt so Western. It was a warm May morning, and would grow hotter as the day progressed. Heading for the center of the small town, she was soon on the wooden sidewalk that marked Main Street.

Kelly entered the local general store and felt as if she'd stepped back in time. The wooden floor was unevenly worn and creaking, totally unlike the sterile linoleum of the supermarkets she was used to. The shelves, tables and counters were loaded with everything a person could need, from jeans and boots to beans and sausage. It had none of the sleek, streamlined look of a supermarket, yet carried a wide range of products. Kelly took a deep breath. The slightly musty smell was unique and she knew she'd always visualize this place in the future by the scent alone.

Molly had introduced Kelly to the owner, Beth Stapleton, when she'd first arrived. Beth was in the rear of the store, talking with another young woman. The customer was a few years younger than Beth, younger even than Kelly. Both women were dressed in similar jeans and cotton checked tops. Kelly felt at ease as she headed toward the rear of the store to join them.

"Hi, Kelly, come on back. Here's someone I don't think you've met yet." Beth called a welcome.

Kelly was amazed at the recognition, at the cheery reception. Such a thing rarely happened in San Francisco.

"Kelly Adams, this is Sally Lockford."

Kelly's eyes widened at the name, color receding a little from her cheeks. Disappointment unexpectedly coursed through her. *He was married.* Why hadn't she thought of that? She had assumed he was single. Yet Molly had talked as if his hell-raising days were gone. She should have guessed why.

Masking her feelings, Kelly smiled politely and replied. Studying the other woman, Kelly realized she was not long out of her teens. Tall and slim, she had rich, honey blond hair, not pale, white-blond like Kelly's. Her eyes were gray, not blue.

So this was the woman who had tamed the hell-raiser. How had she done it? She looked quiet and shy and far too young.

"I'm so pleased to meet you," Sally said. "I bought one of your books for my niece's last birthday. *Amy and the Giant Pancake.*"

"That one was fun. Just right for little girls, I thought." Kelly smiled. It was always nice to hear praise about her work.

"Are you working on another one now?" Sally asked.

"Yes. In fact, Beth, that's why I'm here. I'm having trouble sketching a pony. I can't get the pictures right—the pony seems too stiff. I wondered if you could introduce me to someone who has horses? Maybe I could go and watch them in action, get a better feel for how horses move."

"Would a real pony do? We have one for the kids," Sally said. "We'd love to have you use ours as a model."

Kelly looked at Sally in surprise. There were children? She must be older than she looked. Again she felt a sinking within her, a wave of disappointment. She should have known better. He was too handsome and exciting to still be single. And she was foolish beyond belief to think he would want to see her again, based on one shouting match in the middle of the street.

"Good idea," Beth agreed. "Ponies are usually stockier than horses, shorter legs. You'd get a better perspective, Kelly, using an actual pony."

"That's very kind," Kelly replied slowly. Now that she could see Kit Lockford again, it would be in his home with his wife and children. The prospect was no longer appealing.

"Good, it's settled." Sally glanced at her watch. "I'm going to have to go. Kit drove me in and he'll be wanting to leave soon. I'll wait out front for him. I don't like to keep him waiting." Sally gathered her packages and started for the door, Beth and Kelly walking alongside.

"Speaking of Kit, did you hear about the run-in he had with Kelly?" Beth asked mischievously.

"No, what happened?" Sally looked at Beth, then at Kelly.

"Beth," Kelly protested, but to deaf ears. Beth proceeded to relate the entire incident, suitably embellished to Kelly's advantage. Kelly didn't know how to handle small-town gossip, especially when she was the center of it. In future she'd have to keep that in mind before she started yelling at anyone in public.

Sally turned to Kelly with wide eyes. "How did you dare? You look so delicate and feminine. And Kit is so awesome when he's mad."

Kelly pulled a face. "So am I."

"I'm impressed. Just wait until I tell Clint. He'll love it. Come to our place tomorrow, Kelly, to see the pony."

Kelly had second thoughts, but couldn't think of a reason to refuse when she'd just asked Beth for help.

"Sally, why don't you go over to Kelly's place now, and write out the directions for her. You can see some of the changes she's made since she's been here. She's brightened up the place and it looks really nice, Molly said. I'll let Kit know where you are when he comes."

Sally agreed, and she and Kelly started back toward the old Victorian house near the edge of town. "It still seems odd not to have Margaret on the porch as we drive by," Sally murmured as they walked on the wooden sidewalk. "I'm sorry about her death."

"I never knew her. Actually, I didn't even know she existed until she was gone," Kelly replied wistfully. "I wish I had. I always wanted some family. I was orphaned young."

"Well, families aren't necessarily all they're cracked up to be. Look at the one I'm in," Sally said darkly. "Though I'm lucky to have Clint."

"Clint?"

"My husband, Clint Lockford," Sally answered.

Kelly looked at her in surprise. "I thought Kit was your husband."

"Good grief, no! Kit's not married. I can't even imagine such a thing! Anyway, he's ages older than I am. Clint and I have been married for a year now. He's a darling."

Kelly suddenly felt lighter, happier. She didn't stop to analyze why; enough to know Kit Lockford was not married and that she might be seeing him soon.

They walked the short distance to Kelly's house where Sally duly admired the changes Kelly had made. The house was brighter, with windows and curtains open to the sun and fresh air, rather than closed to preserve the furniture as her aunt had apparently kept it.

Sally wrote careful, precise directions to the ranch, giving them to Kelly with a renewed invitation for the next afternoon.

An impatient horn from the driveway had her springing up from the kitchen table nervously.

"It's Kit. I've got to go." Sally scrambled for her parcels. Kelly picked up a couple of packages and walked with her out to the truck, curious to see Mr. Kit Lockford again.

His hat was low on his face, his hands tapping an impatient tattoo on the steering wheel. He made no effort to get out and help his sister-in-law, just watched the two women descend the three wooden steps from Kelly's porch and walk down to the dirt driveway, his face impassive.

On the bottom stair Kelly's gaze clashed with his. Light blue eyes to dark stormy ones. Kelly lost awareness of Sally, of the rough walkway, the summer heat, everything as she returned his hard, compelling stare. Her breath constricted in her throat and she could feel the heated blood pound through her veins as each step brought her closer to him. She didn't look away, drawn to him as a moth to a flame.

Sally tossed her packages into the back, took the ones Kelly carried and added them.

"Thanks, see you tomorrow." She hastily went around the rear of the truck and climbed into the cab.

"Hi," Kelly said saucily, still impaled by Kit's gaze. She refused to cower around this arrogant man, wanting to see if she could provoke another reaction. She hoped he couldn't hear her racing heart. Determined she would not be the first to look away, she kept her eyes firmly on his, seeing the shifting emotions as he met her gaze.

Tilting her chin a little, Kelly let a trace of mockery enter her own eyes. Time someone took Mr. Lockford to task for his arrogance. And just maybe she was that someone.

Kit ignored her greeting, but his eyes left hers to insolently trail down her figure, lingering on her high, firm breasts clearly defined by her cotton top, again on her narrow waist and on the long legs lovingly molded by snug jeans. When his eyes met hers again they were hot with hunger and something else.

Kelly flushed, her nerves tingling as if he'd touched her. Then anger flashed. The nerve of the man. Who did he think he was? That was the second time she'd let him get to her. She longed for some scathing comment that would put him in his place. But the slamming of the passenger door drew Kit's attention and the moment was lost.

"Sally's brave. I admire her," Kelly said softly, determined he'd not leave without speaking to her.

When Kit's eyes swung back to her, she smiled sweetly. "Imagine being brave enough to ride with you, Taylorville's own Paul Newman." Her voice was as soft as silk.

He frowned. "What do you mean?"

"He's a race driver, like you. And he has sexy blue eyes, just like you." Her look was pure sassiness.

He put the truck in reverse and backed swiftly out, tires squealing, without another word to Kelly. His face was closed and hard.

"Drive safely now," she called sweetly.

Watching as he drove off, Kelly was rewarded by one last quick glance from Kit Lockford. He scowled even more as she smiled gleefully, triumphantly at his look and gave him a saucy wave. Cheered by his last action, she turned back to her house, honors about even.

Two

Damn, but she was sassy, Kit thought as he drove down the highway, his adrenaline pumping as it hadn't in quite some time. He'd like to shut her sassy mouth. Preferably with his. Bring color to her cheeks from passion rather than from anger. His hands tightened on the steering wheel, though he wished they could tighten around that smart-mouth blonde back in town.

He hadn't felt like this about a woman in years. Why that young madam? Who was she? Beth had mentioned her name—Kelly Adams. But nothing more.

He ignored his sister-in-law as he drove, his expression tight as he battled forgotten feelings and long-buried yearnings. He hadn't had a woman in years and suddenly he was aching for one he'd seen only twice. He wanted her with a surprising intensity, brought about by abstinence, undoubtedly. He hadn't planned to see her again. Though maybe he had, if he was honest. Why else would he have volunteered to drive Sally into town today? He flicked a glance at his young sister-in-law, huddled by the door, gazing out the window. She was so timid, almost afraid around him. He tightened his lips and looked straight ahead. Then they softened slightly as he remembered Kelly Adams. She wasn't afraid of him. And from her attitude today, she still didn't know about him. He smiled grimly.

Her attitude hadn't changed from their first encounter. She was bold, sassy, challenging. Why hadn't they told her about him? Where was the pity, the damned compassion that made him feel like an invalid, like half a man? He felt as if he'd been given a reprieve. At least until next time.

Now he knew where she lived. He'd been surprised when Beth Stapleton had told him Sally was at Kelly's house, and pointed it out to him. Kelly. A nice name. Was she Irish? She sure had a temper. He almost smiled. She seemed easy to rile. And then she almost spit fire. Would she be as passionate in bed?

With a groan he dragged his thoughts away. The last thing she'd ever want was to be in bed with him.

"Are you all right, Kit?" Sally asked, turning to look at him.

Flushing slightly, he nodded. "Who's the blonde?" He'd find out what he could about her. Maybe find out she was already taken, not that it would make any difference to him. There couldn't be anything between them even if she wasn't taken.

"Kelly Adams is the author of *Amy and the Giant Pancake,* that book I got for Julie at her last birthday, remember?"

He frowned. She was a writer?

"Umm." He remembered. He'd read the book to the little girl a dozen times or more during her last visit. "She here for a visit?"

"She inherited Margaret Palmer's house. She's Margaret's great-niece. I think she's moved here for good. Wouldn't that be exciting?"

He smiled at Sally. He knew she was nervous around him, afraid of his temper. But he liked his brother's wife and would never harm her.

"Yeah, exciting. Does her family like Taylorville?" Had his tone been casual enough? Would she guess he was trying to find out some more about the pretty newcomer?

"She's alone, as far as Beth knows. Beth met her a few days ago when she first moved in. Molly Benson brought her by. She's pretty, isn't she?" Sally asked, watching him carefully.

"Molly?"

Sally giggled. "No, Kelly Adams."

He shrugged. "Pretty enough." There was no denying that, and to do so would raise speculation. He sighed softly as he turned in to the ranch. It didn't matter. He'd do better to stay home in the future, avoid further run-ins with pretty Kelly Adams. It would be safer for him.

Kelly was ready to leave for the Lockford ranch much too early the next afternoon. She'd chosen jeans for the ranch, and a light blue cotton knit shirt because it brought out the clear blue of her eyes. She had a nice figure, and the casual clothes displayed it to advantage. Not that she cared, she told herself as she examined how the top hugged her breasts, the jeans molded her bottom. But her body began to tingle in growing anticipation, remembering Kit's raking looks. She licked dry lips.

Unable to wait any longer, Kelly started out, carefully following Sally's directions. They were clear and simple and soon Kelly turned onto the access road for the ranch.

The rolling grassland flanked the narrow lane as it twisted and turned, following a natural valley. When the valley gradually widened it gave way to a long plateau. The Lockford home was straight ahead, a low, rambling, one-story stucco house with a red tile roof and lots of large windows. A wide wooden deck spanned the front, three shallow stairs leading up to the front door, and an incline of some sort at the far end. To the right, behind the house, was a large faded red barn, the corral at the side occupied by several horses dozing in the sun. Smaller buildings dotted the flat portion of the land. Beyond the structures, the grassy hills rose and fell. Cattle grazed in the distance. She could almost hear the silence.

Kelly drew up beside two large pickups near the deck. The blue-and-white one she recognized immediately. Did that mean Kit was home? Now that she might run into him again, she was nervous. Brushing her hands against her jeans, she climbed out and walked up to the front door.

It stood wide open, a screen door preventing entry of unwanted insects. Kelly rapped on the frame. The afternoon was still and quiet. She turned to look around her, at the silent hills, the tranquillity of the ranch. She had expected more activity. Was everyone out on the range?

Kelly rapped again, and heard a curious thumping. Then a familiar voice, deep, drawling and lazy, called out. It sounded different when not tinged with anger.

"Come in. The door isn't locked."

She entered the house and found herself in a long hallway, dim after the bright sunlight. Ahead she saw a tall figure outlined against a window at the far end.

"Hi." She was more nervous than she'd thought she'd be. How long before her eyes adjusted? Where was Sally?

"What are you doing here?" he asked, moving closer.

"Gracious as ever, I see," she said, standing taller. She'd been right. Kit Lockford was a tall man, shoulders broad, chest strong and full. His waist was lean, tapering to slim hips, his long legs covered by tight denims. She feasted her eyes on him as they adjusted to the light. He looked masculine, powerful and sexy as hell.

He was also on crutches. That stopped her in surprise.

"Did you sprain your ankle?" she asked.

His eyes narrowed. "Very funny. I asked why you're here." His tone was sharp.

"Sally invited me. I'm here to see the pony."

"Aren't you a little old for a pony?"

"I want to draw it, not ride it. Though I always wished I had a pony as a child." She blushed as she turned away. Why blurt out something like that, especially to someone who didn't like her? She needed to watch her tongue or he'd think she was an idiot.

He seemed to tower over her, disapproving. She glanced up into his face, her smile fading as tension rose in the hallway. His hair was brown, with strands of burnished gold bleached by the sun. His skin was deeply tanned from the long California summers. His eyes were hard to see in the faint light, but she knew they were a deep, dark blue. He stared down at her, his lips thin and his expression remote, almost bleak.

She resisted a strong urge to reach out and brush her hands against his arm, his chest. Her fingers ached to touch him, and she clenched her hands around her sketch pad to keep from giving in to the urge.

"Sally's out in the barn. Anyone outside can show you the pony."

"I'm Kelly Adams." She was reluctant to leave.

"I know, I've heard an earful about you from Sally. Children's books bore me," he said flatly, his eyes never leaving hers.

She was taken aback. "Yes, I suppose they do most adults, Mr. Lockford. But I hope mine don't bore children," she replied with dignity. "I'll find Sally." She thought her legs would give way her knees were so shaky. As she pushed back through the screen door and started toward the old barn she tried to keep from giving in to tears. Damn, he was downright rude! There was no reason to insult her work. She would never attack someone's livelihood. If she did, he'd be the first she'd tell about what she thought about cowboys. Half the time they were little boys who couldn't grow up, forever playing cowboys and Indians. He needn't act so superior

Though there was nothing of a little boy about Kit Lockford. Just once she'd like to get the better of him!

Her anger and hurt were forgotten as she walked toward the barn looking around her in interest. There was so much to see. Four horses dozed in the corral, three sleek chestnuts and a spotted Appaloosa. Kelly veered to the rail and peered through the bars. She'd be content to stand and watch the beautiful creatures for hours on end. She wanted to capture their grace and beauty in her sketches. Wanted her illustrations for the new book to be as perfect as she could get them.

"Kelly, hello." Sally came from the barn, a smile of welcome on her face.

"Hi, Sally. They're beautiful," Kelly said, turning back to the animals.

"Thanks. Come on inside. Clint's there, you can meet him. Then we'll get Popo."

Kelly followed Sally, her gaze darting everywhere. Empty stalls lined both walls of the big barn. A massive loft for winter hay storage was overhead. At the far end a man groomed a fine black gelding. As Kelly drew near, she knew he had to be Clint. He was a younger version of his brother.

He was tall, with curly chestnut hair and the same broad shoulders. But his smile was wide and friendly, not arrogant and sexy. And his voice was warm with welcome.

"I hear Popo's going to be the role model for a new book?"

"I hope so. I got the idea for the story when I saw a black pony in a field, on the other side of town. But I need to see movement, get a better idea of how ponies move. I try to do realistic work, even if it is only for kids." Was she justifying her own work now, just because of Kit's words?

"We enjoyed your book about Amy," he said easily. "I must have read it to Julie a dozen times."

"And Kit even more. She couldn't get enough of it," Sally added with a friendly smile.

"I met, um, Kit at the house. I stopped there first. He said it bored him," Kelly said lightly, shyly reaching out to pat the sleek neck of the horse standing so docilely.

Clint chuckled. "It probably did after the eight millionth time. Julie was thrilled with it. I liked the pictures. I felt as if I was there."

"Come on, I'll show you Popo," Sally said. She led the way to the back corral, where two more horses looked up with interest as the women arrived. In the far corner was a small cream-colored pony, with a long, silky, blond mane and tail. Kelly was enchanted, though Popo didn't have the lost, sad look she saw with the black pony.

"Clint bought him for my niece and nephews, for when they visit. He gets ridden a lot when they're here. Other than that, he's got it made. Food twice a day and no other responsibilities."

"Great life." Kelly smiled. She opened her tablet and began sketching the pony while he stood in the sun, moved across the corral, drank from the trough.

Sally then led him around on a lead rope, put him through different gaits while Kelly watched carefully, sketching the different movements. It was perfect. This was exactly what she needed. She had a much better feel for how the pony moved.

The afternoon flew by. Kelly finally reluctantly gathered her things. "I should be going." She gave a fond look at the little pony, now eating from the hay a cowboy had tossed in the corral a few minutes ago.

"Stay for dinner," Sally suggested. "We're having chicken and I have plenty to go around."

"I'd like that," Kelly agreed after a moment's thought. She'd get to see Kit again. Would he be disagreeable around his brother and sister-in-law? "Can I help?"

"Sure. I like company in the kitchen. Clint usually comes in then and sits with me as I cook." Sally smiled shyly. "We've not been married all that long. Being apart all day, it's nice to be together in the evening even if it's only to cook supper."

"I think that's nice. How long have you two been married?"

"Just a year last month. We wanted to get married before that, but weren't sure how it'd work with Kit and all. It's turned out fine," she said quickly.

It must be difficult to start married life living with your in-laws. Couldn't Clint afford a separate house for him and

Sally? Was it Kit's house? Not that it was any of her business, but she was curious.

The two women worked easily together, laughing as they fried the chicken, set out beverages and baked biscuits. Clint joined them as they worked, tilted back in one of the kitchen chairs, joining in the fun and laughter. He helped by setting the dining-room table and carrying in the food. When it was on the table, he went to the hall to yell for Kit.

Kit Lockford arrived silently, gliding in a wheelchair.

Kelly's eyes widened in surprise. That explained the absence of a chair at the foot of the table. She was surprised at the wheelchair, however. Usually sprained ankles weren't serious enough for a wheelchair. Maybe it was broken.

"Well, well, I see Miss Goodness-and-Light is dining with us," Kit said as he maneuvered the chair deftly in place, his eyes on Kelly.

"Kit," Clint said with an edge to his voice.

But Kelly wasn't cowed. "Well, well, still the arrogant macho cowboy, I see. Your mother should have taught you some manners when you were a kid," she replied, giving him a false sweet smile.

His eyes lit appreciably, and a smile almost reached his lips. "And yours should have taught you to watch your tongue when visiting in a man's house."

"I never really knew my mother, but I'm sure she would have told me to stand up to egotistical and conceited males. Anyway," she said graciously, "I expect you feel out of sorts if your ankle ached."

"Ankle?" Sally looked puzzled, glancing between Kit and Kelly.

"Didn't he hurt his ankle?" Kelly looked at Sally. "I asked when I first arrived." She looked back suspiciously at Kit. "You didn't deny it."

He made no response, but a devilish glint entered his eyes as he stared at her, holding her gaze.

"Oh, Kelly," Sally said softly, sadly. "Kit was in a bad accident a couple of years ago. He's partially paralyzed.

That's why he uses crutches. He can't walk without them.''
Sally trailed off.

Kelly's eyes clashed with his in sudden realization. How
awful! And how he must hate it! He was so strong, active,
virile. God, to be confined to a wheelchair must be hell for
anyone, but how much worse for a rancher, a man used to
roaming endless acres of land, riding horses, walking his
property. How could he stand the loss of such freedom? Her
stomach tightened in painful sympathy and she swallowed
hard.

"I'm sorry, I didn't know," she said matter-of-factly.
"You could have told me." She still faced Kit. She refused
to be embarrassed, as she was sure he'd deliberately misled
her. He'd known she hadn't known he was paralyzed and
had deliberately hidden the situation from her. Why? To
have her make a fool of herself? Well, she was sorry, but she
refused to be upset with her error. He could have set her
straight.

Kit sat back, searching her eyes for the pity and compassion he always found. But he didn't see it in Kelly. She was
still staring at him but she looked as if she was getting angry again. He glanced at his brother and Sally, then back to
Kelly. Her gaze was almost furious.

"No reason you should know," he said.

"No, just let me make a fool of myself thinking you'd
sprained your ankle. Do you like people making themselves look foolish?"

He shrugged. "It's a change."

Her lips tightened as tension rose. Oh! She'd like to slap
that tanned face and get some response out of him beyond
the bored indifference. It was a wonder he wasn't laughing
himself silly at the way he'd fooled her.

"Have some chicken, Kit." Sally offered the loaded plate,
trying to soothe the situation. "Kelly helped me with it."

"I wonder if I dare eat any," he said, reaching for the
platter.

"You can," Kelly assured him earnestly. "I'll point out
the poisoned pieces so you won't miss them."

His eyes gleamed, but before he could reply, Clint asked Kelly where she was from and how she liked living in ranch country, obviously trying to defuse the situation. She answered his questions, conscious of Kit's silent regard throughout the meal.

Sally told them what they'd done with the pony that afternoon, and raved about Kelly's sketches.

"So Popo worked out okay?" Clint asked.

"Yes, it's been very helpful. But he doesn't look sad, like my little black pony. The one I'm writing the book about."

"Which one is that?"

"I don't know. I saw him alone in a field when I was exploring one of the side roads. He was just standing near a tree and looked so sad." She paused and shot a quick glance at Kit. Surely that was the perfect opening for another of his sarcastic remarks. Cowboys probably didn't think ponies looked sad or happy.

"Smiths', I bet." Kit answered his brother, ignoring Kelly. "I heard they got one for their grandchild."

"The baby's only six months old," Sally said.

"Probably why the thing's sad," Kit scoffed, catching Kelly's eye, teasing lights dancing in his. "I know where he's kept. I'll take you to see him sometime, if you like," he tossed off the words.

Kelly couldn't believe her ears. Was that a genuine offer? Quickly before he could change his mind she accepted.

From time to time as the meal continued she glanced at Kit, trying to determine what made him tick. He contributed little to the conversation, though whenever she looked at him, his eyes were on her—hard, dark, glittering. Rather than make her nervous, it was exhilarating.

When he'd finished eating, Kit excused himself and silently glided from the room. From the resigned look between Sally and Clint, Kelly suspected this was his normal behavior. She was disappointed when he left, though she knew he wouldn't stay just to spend time with her.

As soon as the dishes were finished, Kelly planned to leave.

"Don't go yet," Sally said. "It's still early."

"Not really, it's already dark outside. I'm new enough to worry about the drive home. It's a lot different from San Francisco. I've enjoyed the afternoon and evening, Sally. Thank you. I've got some great sketches of the pony. It's been a huge help."

"I'm glad you came. Will we see you at the dance next Saturday?"

"What dance?"

"A Memorial Day celebration, with dancing and food galore. There'll be a small band, ladies bring food, guys chip in for the beer and cokes. Oh, Kelly, please come. It's a lot of fun and you'll get to meet everyone."

When Kelly agreed to go, Sally gave her the particulars.

She didn't see Clint or Kit again, but asked Sally to tell them goodbye as she started out. It was dark with no moon, and no streetlights. The driveway from the Lockford house was long and narrow. She drove carefully, not wanting to drive off the pavement. Reaching the highway without mishap, she breathed a sigh of relief as she turned toward home.

The highway was dark and deserted until a car came right up behind her, the headlights higher than her compact car, the glare in the mirror blinding. She adjusted her mirror down, slowed to let the other car pass. It slowed, as well. Kelly had heard stories of people attacked on long, lonely stretches of rural highway. The other driver would be able to see she was alone. A flicker of fear ran through her. She sped up. The car behind her kept pace.

Kelly strained to see the lights of town. It couldn't be too far. It hadn't taken her long to reach the Lockford place that afternoon. The bright lights of the other car filled hers, keeping her constantly aware of the following vehicle. They were alone on the highway. What if he ran her off the road? Ran into her car? God, where was the town?

She caught a glimmer of light in the distance. Speeding up a little, she soon saw the lights of the houses and the general store. Almost home. She'd be all right, just a little farther.

Slowing for her driveway, she turned in, safe at last.

The other vehicle turned in behind her. Her heart lurched as it stopped just behind her car. She eyed the distance to her door. Could she make a dash for it, have her key ready and get safely inside before the other driver reached her? Her shoulders sagged. There would not be enough time. And using her key would give the other person a few seconds advantage.

Could she make it to Molly's house? Pound on her door, at least let someone know she needed help? She glanced in the mirror. Had the other driver already gotten out?

Suddenly Kelly threw open her door, slammed it shut and stalked directly into the headlights, swerving to come up alongside the high blue-and-white truck.

"Do you know you scared me half to death?" she said through gritted teeth, looking into the dark cab at the figure dimly illuminated by the dashboard lights.

"Just wanted to make sure you got home safely," came the lazy drawl.

"I can take care of myself, thank you."

"Just trying to be neighborly." Was there a hint of amusement in his voice? Did he think it funny she had been practically terrified? If so, he had a sick sense of humor!

"How was I to know who you were?"

He flicked off his headlights, plunging them into darkness. "Why don't you yell louder," he said softly, "so all your neighbors will hear you?"

Kelly glanced around. She saw no one.

"I wasn't yelling," she said in a lower tone, knowing she had been. He always put her on the defensive. Had he really followed her due to concern? A small warmth touched her heart. No one had ever worried about her before. Not that she could remember.

"Do you want to come in for a cup of coffee?" she offered, reluctant to have him leave, dying to learn more about Kit Lockford.

He didn't reply at once, and she could almost feel him weighing the pros and cons of such a move. At last he spoke. "Okay, I'll try it."

"I've heard more eager acceptances from people going to the dentist," she muttered. "What are you going to try, the coffee? Afraid I might poison it?"

"No, I'll try the experience of drinking it with a sassy-mouthed termagant."

"I am not." Her voice raised again.

"For all you look like an angel, you have the temper of a shrew and the stubbornness of a mule. You take the cake when complaining about my behavior."

Kelly didn't know what to say. He'd said she looked like an angel. She smiled, liking the compliment. For the moment she'd ignore the rest of his comment.

"Come in for coffee," she said softly.

Kit opened the door and swung his legs out. The crutches were drawn from the seat and he eased out until he was standing.

"I'll shut the door," she said as he began his slow way to her house. Her heart went out to him as he moved slowly along the uneven walkway. Afraid one or the other crutch would not find a secure place, afraid he'd fall, she hovered alongside, watching the path and Kit, hoping her reflexes would be fast enough.

He stopped abruptly and looked down at her.

"I can manage fine if you'll stop dithering around me. What do you think you're going to do if I fall? Cushion the blow? You certainly couldn't hold me up."

"I was trying to help," she snapped, stalking ahead. "Don't call me if you fall on your face and don't yell and bother the neighbors." She flounced up the three steps to her porch and opened the door. Glancing back briefly she added, "And I'm very strong."

She went down her hall to the kitchen, switching on lights so Kit could find his way. Her temper boiled again. *Dithering!* She had not been dithering. Was it so wrong to want to help?

Flinging her sketch pad on the table, Kelly filled the kettle and placed it on the stove. Kit came in slowly and sank onto one of her chairs, his crutches clattering loudly to the floor.

Kelly jumped and turned to glare at him, knowing he'd done it deliberately. She was as nervous around him as a girl being asked to a prom. Then she smiled. If she were pleasant, it would throw him off guard, make him mad. "I have some cake. Would you care for some?"

"No, just coffee'll be fine." Taking off his hat, Kit put it on the chair beside him, running his fingers through his thick hair. He fingered the sketch pad, pulling it over and ruffling through it. Closing it, he tossed it carelessly aside. Kelly was piqued when he made no comment on the drawings, but refused to show it.

The silence stretched out awkwardly.

"How did you hurt yourself?" Kelly asked at last.

He looked up, his eyes narrowing. "I didn't hurt myself. I became paralyzed from a bull," he stated clearly.

She poured the hot water over the coffee grounds and waited while it dripped. She wondered what the bull had been doing and why Kit hadn't gotten out of the way.

"Both legs?" she asked, her eyes on the coffee slowly filling the carafe.

"Partially. That's the only reason I can maneuver with the crutches. Otherwise I'd be confined to that damned wheelchair all the time."

"Frustrating, I bet." She was careful to keep all signs of sympathy from her voice.

"You Mrs. Freud?"

"No, but you look like an active, physical man. The limitation must be frustrating."

Kelly looked down at her hands, wondering at the desire she had to smooth the lines of pain from his face, thread her fingers through his thick, springing hair and hold him close to her for comfort. He was the last man in the world to want comfort. Especially from her. Yet she wanted to give it.

She swirled around and saw the coffee was ready. Her hands shook slightly as she poured it, and she only hoped he didn't notice.

"Do you raise cattle on your ranch?" She strove for a neutral topic, something they could discuss without the tension and strain they had found at each meeting. She didn't want to be angry anymore. She wanted to learn about him, his life.

"Yeah, Herefords. We have a large herd. I do the paperwork now, Clint ramrods the cowboys."

"How many?"

"We've got a half dozen fellows that work for us all year long, and hire on extra when mustering for market. You interested in ranching?"

"Just trying to learn what I can about the places around here. It's all different and new to me. I've always lived in San Francisco before."

Kit seemed to relax in the pleasant kitchen and began talking briefly about his ranch. His short, descriptive phrases painted a practical picture of cattle ranching, and Kelly was an avid listener. She wasn't shy about asking questions if he lost her, or when she wanted more information. It was a fascinating way of life, especially to one born and raised in the city.

He drained his cup and set it down. Reaching for his hat, he looked at her.

"Thanks for the coffee."

"Thanks for seeing me home," she said, feeling suddenly shy. "Next time let me know it's you following."

"There may not be a next time now that I know how capable you are," he drawled, his eyes on her mouth.

Three

Kit stared at her for an endless moment as time seemed suspended. He longed to feel those soft lips against his. Feel the heat he knew was in her, the passion her fiery words promised. In the past he'd never hesitated, never questioned. He took what he wanted, giving pleasure as he sampled women the way most men only dreamed of. But that had all changed two long years ago.

He hadn't touched a woman since Althea. Gone was the carefree, cocky cowboy of the old days, for all Kelly apparently thought differently. In his place now was a cripple. A man who was only partially a man, scarred and limited. *No one wants to be tied to a cripple*. The hateful words Althea had screamed at him in the hospital echoed over and over. He turned from the temptation of Kelly Adams and reached for his crutches. Jamming his hat on his head, he slowly stood, steadied himself and started for the door.

"You've done your good deed for the week, Miss Adams," he said mockingly as he started down the hall.

"What does that mean?" Kelly followed slowly, reluctant to have the evening end, knowing he should go before she did something silly, like ask him to stay. Like ask him to kiss her. She didn't even know the man. But she wanted to.

"Come on, pretty lady, the last thing you wanted tonight was some cripple going on and on about a cattle spread that is only nominally his anymore." He couldn't hide the bitterness. Though the fault was his own, he hated the twist of fate that had landed him in this situation. Hated it even more the past few days than before.

She reached out and stopped his progress toward the door with a warm hand on his arm. He swung around and cocked an eyebrow in question.

Kelly tilted her head to see him better as he took a step closer. Stepping away from his overwhelming masculinity, she backed against the wall, acutely aware of the smoky hue of his eyes, aware of the tension radiating between them. She was unable to look away as she felt herself melting in a dark blue gaze that devoured her. Her heart began a shudderingly slow pounding. She could feel the heat from his body encompass her as she leaned against the wall. When he stepped even closer, her tongue darted out between her lips to moisten them.

He leaned toward her, his eyes narrowed in consideration. "One good shove will knock me down, if that's what you want." He waited a second, then slowly lowered his head and put his mouth over hers.

Kelly trembled slightly at the delight of his touch, releasing a soft sigh. His lips were warm and firm, provoking an unexpectedly deep response from her. Her knees grew weak and she was glad of the wall behind her for support. His touch was melting her through and through.

When he felt her response, he pressed against her. His hard chest crushed against her breasts, his long legs moved to capture hers. His lips opened hers to tease her into a deeper kiss. When his tongue explored the soft reaches of her mouth, he heard a faint moan from her throat. He felt her shyly open her mouth wider, giving him permission for whatever he wanted from her.

The weight of his body pressing against hers was heaven. Her hands brushed against his chest, over his strong arms, moving, questing, as they found the strong column of his neck, and at last felt the springy texture of his hair. Threading it in her fingers, she held him close to her, acknowledging the deepening kiss.

She delighted in the sweetness of his thrusting tongue, his lips moving in sensuous satisfaction against her soft flesh. She lost all concept of time, drowning in endless delight and floating bliss. She strained to get closer, moving her lips against his, her hands pressing, his mouth hard against hers, her body molding itself against the length of his.

Endless moments passed before Kit eased his mouth from hers and raised his head. His eyes half closed, he watched her lazily as he slowly straightened and stepped awkwardly back on his crutches.

"That was better than any cake," he said as he turned and started toward the door again.

Kelly hadn't moved, looking at him with bewildered eyes. Why had he stopped? She could have gone on forever. She traced her still-warm lips with her tongue, tasting Kit. She felt cold and alone with him gone. Her arms ached to hold him, her mouth ached for his. But he walked away.

Pushing away from the wall, Kelly followed him to the door, standing there to watch as he made his way to his truck. He never looked back. Lightly tracing her lips again, she watched the red lights of the truck fade in the distance.

God, I'll have to watch myself, he thought as the town lights disappeared behind him. She was so sweet, so feminine, so damned tempting. Yet she wasn't shy and timid like Sally. She gave as good as she got. He smiled, remembering some of the things she'd said to him, starting with that first day when she'd called him an idiot. She had a mouth on her.

Hell, he'd prove he was an idiot if he continued. There was nothing he could offer her. Forget the hot kisses. He needed to return to the way things had been before he met her. He'd stay on the ranch and ignore her. And she'd forget him before long.

The decision did nothing to improve his mood.

Sally Lockford called Kelly Friday morning.

"I'm going to get a new dress for the dance tomorrow, so I'm coming to town. Kit's going to drive me in. Want to have lunch at the café?"

"I'd like to have lunch together, but why don't you eat here? Kit, too, of course." Kelly smiled in secret glee at the prospect of seeing him again. He'd been constantly in her thoughts. And she had wondered how to arrange a meeting again. Had he thought of her even once?

"I'd love to. I can't speak for Kit, though. He's been grouchy as can be this last week, worse than usual," Sally said.

"Well, the invitation is open if he wants to join us."

Kelly hoped he'd stop for lunch, but Kit only dropped Sally off just before noon and roared down the street with the same disregard for others on the road as he had displayed the first time Kelly saw him. Not wanting Sally to suspect the extent of her fascination with Kit, Kelly merely commented that she was sorry he couldn't stay.

Sally left after lunch to look for a dress. Kelly sat out on her front porch, watching in case Kit didn't see Sally in town and came back by Kelly's place. Actually, she was hoping he'd miss his sister-in-law in town and stop by. She was rewarded when she heard the throaty growl of his engine. Kelly hurried to the driveway as he turned in.

He sat in the truck, motor running, watching her approach with brooding eyes. Even when she smiled, he did not. Did he ever greet people? Smile? Wave? she wondered. It didn't matter, she was glad to see him, for however brief a time.

"Hi," she said brightly.

"Where's Sally?"

"Fine, thank you, and you?" Putting her hands on the open window as if to hold the truck in place, Kelly responded as if he'd asked how she was. "Don't you say hello when you see anyone?"

"Why?"

"It's polite."

"Hello. Where's Sally?"

"She went to get the dress for the dance. I think she's at Beth's. Are you going to the dance?"

"Now why would a cripple who can't even walk go to a dance?" his insolent voice asked her as he flicked his glance over her before turning away. He put the truck in reverse and released the brake. The truck began rolling slowly back toward the highway. Kelly walked along, her hands still on the window.

"I thought it was a social gathering to celebrate Memorial Day. Couldn't you come for that?"

He shook his head. "Take your hands away. I don't want you to get hurt."

She stepped back and watched him drive away, wondering if it was already too late to worry about getting hurt. Too much of her time was taken in thinking about Kit Lockford. She dwelt on their meetings, thinking up different, clever things she should have said. Remembering their kiss. Remembering how he made her feel. How she wanted to kiss him again. The feelings he caused her were unlike any she'd ever experienced before. They were heady, exciting, sexy, and she wanted to experience them again.

Kelly waited on her front porch until Kit and Sally passed on their way home. Kit didn't look her way, and Kelly was disappointed. Maybe he didn't feel the same spark of attraction she felt so strongly between them. Maybe it was just her. She looked down the road long after they'd disappeared, remembering his kisses and the anticipation and delight she'd experienced around him each time. Didn't he feel any of the sensual pull she felt?

* * *

The next evening Kelly took pains with her appearance as she dressed for the dance. This was her first social event in her new town and she wanted to fit in. Forgoing some of the more sophisticated of her dresses, she settled on a light batiste cotton, pale blue and summery. The bodice was snug, the skirt full and flaring. She wore white sandals, which displayed her shapely legs to advantage. Highlighting her eyes, she needed no further makeup. She brushed her hair until it swirled like a soft, wavy cloud around her face. She was still a little nervous, but already knew several people who would be there—Molly, Beth, Sally, Clint. She'd meet others and take another step toward belonging.

She had prepared a double batch of Heavenly Delight, a chewy chocolate cookie, for her contribution. She picked up the wrapped dessert dish and left the house. The school was only a few blocks away so she planned to walk. It just wasn't far enough to drive.

She felt strange walking along the country highway in the twilight. There were no streetlights, no sidewalks. It seemed very desolate, with only an occasional car passing. She quickened her pace when she saw the low brick building illuminated by lights inside and out. There were dozens of cars haphazardly parked around the high school, more arriving every minute.

When she entered, she saw the tables stacked with food along one wall, a bar set up against another. The dance band was at the far end. Folding chairs had been placed around the perimeter. Several couples were already staking a claim to chairs before everyone arrived.

Kelly added her contribution to the already crowded table. Glancing around, she spotted Beth and her husband, Mike, and waved. Joining them, she was soon introduced to friends of Beth's from school days who were reminiscing about the school activities they'd shared in this very gym.

When the music started, Kelly was quickly claimed for a dance by a friend of Beth's. As the evening progressed, the group expanded and contracted as couples joined, drifted away. More and more single men stopped by to meet Kelly, urging Beth or Mike to perform introductions. Most of the men worked on the ranches in the area. Kelly enjoyed dancing, but couldn't help comparing each of her partners to Kit. She wished it was Kit she was dancing with.

Between dances she nibbled on the food, sipped some beer and talked of books, movies and cattle. During the band's first break Mike's eyes widened.

"Well, I'll be damned. Look who came."

Everyone swiveled to see the reason for his comment. Kit, Clint and Sally Lockford entered the gym. Kit was leaning on his crutches, his face impassive, his hat tilted forward. Ignoring the whispers now running around the room as more and more people became aware of his unusual attendance, he calmly surveyed the crowd.

Spotting Beth and Kelly, Clint said something to Sally and Kit. They turned and made their way to the group.

Introductions were made, and Kelly watched as Kit was surrounded by old friends. Men and women from all over the gym came over to speak with him, greeting him warmly. He talked easily with them, moving skillfully around with his crutches.

When the music started again, he turned toward the chairs along the wall, sitting down easily, slipping his hat and crutches beneath his seat. His expression was again impassive as he watched the dancers.

Kelly watched him from the dance floor as friends took turns sitting out with him, talking and laughing easily together.

He didn't seem to know she was there. Except for his brief greeting, he had ignored her. Was he having such a good time? Or was he deliberately ignoring her for another reason? He talked with so many people and seemed to be enjoying himself. She wanted to sit out a dance with him, too. Talk to him, be close to him again.

Thinking up an excuse, she decided to ask him if his offer to take her to see the black pony was still good. But just as she started toward him, Clint claimed her for a dance. "Having fun?"

"Yes. Everyone's been so nice and friendly. It definitely explodes the small-town myth of a closed society."

He chuckled. "It's really a myth to keep city folks from flooding in."

"I was surprised to see Kit. I thought he didn't come to things like this."

Clint glanced over at his brother, then back to Kelly. "He usually doesn't. Though in all fairness, I guess a dance isn't all that fun if you can't join in."

"He can still visit with friends, enjoy the music," Kelly said, her eyes on the man under discussion. He was talking with Sally.

"This is the first time he's come to anything like this since he was injured. He surprised us when he told us he was coming."

"I'm glad he came," Kelly said simply, her eyes still drinking him in.

The song ended. Clint kept hold of her hand, leading her toward Kit. Sally rose as they approached, smiling at her husband.

"Hi, Kit," Kelly said calmly, nodding at Sally as she took her seat. Sally and Clint moved into the next song and Kelly warily turned to the man beside her. Her heart was pounding, though it had proved easier than she'd thought to join him. Now what?

He looked at her long and hard, his eyes bright, the familiar tightness on his face. Then he shrugged, his face relaxing a little.

"Enjoying yourself?" he asked, taking a sip of beer.

"Yes. I've met so many people I can't keep the names straight. Everyone is friendly."

"Not quite everyone," he said softly.

"Well, maybe *friendly* doesn't quite describe you. You're a little harder to get to know," she teased. Then she remembered his kiss. He might be harder to know, but it was worth the difficulty. "Are you glad you came?"

"It wasn't too bad until Sally gave me some bad news. Now I'm going to be put into a damn awkward situation momentarily and I'm trying to figure a way out," he said shortly, looking over the crowd.

"Just by coming here?" She was puzzled. He seemed to be having a good time. What had gone wrong?

"I shouldn't have come."

"Why? Is there anything I can do?" she asked softly, still perplexed by his comments. Somehow she didn't associate problems with Kit Lockford. He was too domineering to give in to petty problems. He'd run roughshod over anything that got in his way. At least, that was how she saw him. But if there was something she could do to help, she wanted to. Would he have come to the dance if she hadn't teased him about it?

"I don't see how you can help." Taking a long drink from his beer, he then twirled it absently in his hands as he again surveyed the crowded room.

Kelly could feel the tension emanating from him. This time it had nothing to do with her, with them. He was worried, upset. Why? And why did he keep scanning the crowd?

"Are you looking for someone in particular?" Kelly asked, looking across the crowded room.

"Why do you ask?"

"You look like you're seeking someone. Or something."

"Someone I'd rather not see," he muttered.

"Who?"

He drew in a deep breath. His eyes again scanned the room. Then he turned and looked at Kelly. Her heart sank at the bleak look in his eyes.

"Hell, you might as well know. Everyone else here does. I was engaged to be married when I was injured. She broke it off and married someone else. Sally found out she's coming here tonight. Alone. I'd like very much not to see her." He gave a short, bitter laugh. "Hell, I'd do anything to avoid it. Except cause Clint and Sally to have to leave early just because I'm a coward."

Kelly blinked at that. Kit Lockford was definitely not a coward.

"If she married someone else, why is she coming here alone? Where's her husband?" Kelly asked.

"I don't know. Sally said she'd heard they'd split. That Althea was free again. Dammit, I shouldn't have come here tonight!" Kit slammed one fist against his thigh, his eyes again scanning the room, his look almost hunted.

Kelly could feel his anguish swamp her enjoyment of the dance.

"Why don't you want to see her? If you two were planning to marry you must have been close. Why not see her again?"

"Because it's one thing to have your life dumped into your lap, and something else again to still be alone years later, as if I'm still awaiting the lady to condescend to notice me again. That's why, dammit!"

Pride. She blinked. It hurt his pride. God knew he didn't have much else, but he had abundant pride and the situation would take that from him. Of course, if he ran out everyone would know and that would be just as humiliating. Her heart lurched.

"I don't think she'd think that," Kelly said.

"I think that's exactly what she'll think. You don't know her. I do," Kit snapped. "Dammit, the last thing I want is pity and charity from Althea Kendricks. Life is hell enough without that."

"Are you kidding? She's probably thanking her lucky stars she didn't marry you. Of all the bad-tempered, arrogant, stubborn men I've ever met, you take the cake."

"I'm not bad tempered." He glared at her, momentarily distracted.

"Could have fooled me." Suddenly she smiled in triumph, her eyes dancing. "You don't deny arrogant and stubborn, I see."

"Sure I do. That goes without saying. I will admit to a certain amount of self-assurance."

She laughed, leaning closer so he could hear her over the band when she said softly, "You act like the world should sit up and roll over for you. If that's not blatant arrogance, I don't know what is."

"I am not arrogant!" Kit brought his face near hers, so near she could feel his breath brush against her cheeks, smell the beer and spicy cologne he used. She was caught by the look on his face, the tight control he exercised. Shakily she licked her lips, mesmerized by the look from Kit's eyes.

His eyes followed the movement of her tongue, a muscle moving in his cheek. He leaned closer and held her gaze.

"Help me, Kelly," he said so quietly she almost didn't hear him.

"Do what?"

"Don't let me be alone when Althea comes."

"What do you want me to do, sit with you?"

"Hell, I don't know." Kit rubbed a hand across his face, leaning back in his chair. "Dumb idea, forget it."

Kelly's face cleared. "I'm to be your girlfriend?" she asked, astonished.

He looked at her warily, not knowing what to expect.

"Just pretend, right?" she asked. Laughing softly at the notion, she noticed his frown and laughed harder, putting her hand on top of his as it rested on his thigh.

"You're so loverlike, darling," she said when she caught her breath, her eyes dancing in amusement. The entire suggestion was funny from one who was so independent and hard and remote. Imagine him asking her for a favor. *This* favor. It was mind-boggling.

But a look at his closed face, set against the coming pain, touched her heart and she sobered immediately.

"I'll help out, if only to have you be nice to me for a little while." Kelly smiled a slow smile at him, watching the tension ease a little from his eyes.

"How nice?" he asked as wariness slowly crept into his own gaze.

Kelly caught her breath. How could anyone have thrown him over just because he didn't walk without help?

"I'll let you know. Deal?"

"Deal." He took her hand in his and waves of energy pulsated up her arm. She looked at him, her amusement giving way to something else. An awareness of the dominant maleness of him spread through her. The desires and feelings he evoked with no effort on his part flooded her body. She felt vulnerable and fragile and very feminine. What was she getting into?

"If the two of you were engaged and she's now left her husband, seems like the perfect time to get back together, not play games," Kelly said, tugging her hand. Kit didn't release it.

"I don't want to. I don't want her even trying. You're the perfect decoy. You're new in town, young, successful, pretty enough to attract anyone." He frowned at that. "You aren't attached right now, are you?"

She shook her head, fascinated by the play of emotion across his face. "Never have been," she said honestly.

"And you'll go through with it?"

She nodded.

"However long she's here?"

She paused a second, then nodded again, wondering how involved they were supposed to be, and how long Althea was planning to stay.

"It won't take Althea long to find out I've just moved here. Won't she be suspicious?" Kelly asked, giving the situation some thought.

"Depending on how good an actress you are, no. Though she might wonder how anyone could be attracted to me." His voice was bitter, his face tormented.

Kelly's fingers tightened around his and she leaned closer, aching to ease the distress so evident in his expression.

"I think you're sexy as hell, Kit Lockford," she said evenly, her eyes looking straight into his.

He shook his head, looking at her as if she'd lost her mind, then a dull flush spread up his neck, touched his cheeks.

Kelly was delighted. She would never have expected such a reaction from the town's hell-raiser. She smiled in enchantment. Althea must have done a real number on him to shake his own self-confidence so badly. He was more man than she could handle, yet he didn't seem to realize it. Could she continue the charade for any length of time? Would her own heart become involved?

"Then give me a smile, sweetheart," Kit said finally. "The music's stopping and Althea just walked in the door."

Kelly swirled around to look. There were several people in and near the door, most of them strangers to her. Which one was Althea? Kelly wasn't left in doubt long as a tall, slim woman with wavy auburn hair turned and found Kit. She spoke to the person beside her, her eyes never leaving Kit, and then walked deliberately over to him. Her thick auburn hair was beautiful, Kelly thought, and the striking clothes she wore gave her a certain elegance missing from the other women at the dance.

Althea paused dramatically a few steps away, holding the moment as people nearby turned to look at her, curious about her meeting with Kit.

"Hello, Kit." Her voice was low and sultry, accompanied by a provocative smile for Kit alone.

Kelly watched quietly, waiting, feeling as if she was on the edge of a deep, dark hole. So this was Althea. Kelly took an immediate dislike to the woman. Knowing what she'd done to Kit was bad enough, but her air of patronization grated on Kelly's sensibilities. Althea didn't fit in with the rest of the crowd. And she was a troublemaker. Kelly knew enough about human nature to recognize that trait immediately.

Kelly's hand ached with the strength of Kit's grip. He took a deep breath and let it out slowly, his voice even as he said, "Hello, Allie. Didn't expect to see you tonight."

Althea smiled brilliantly. "Just visiting my parents for a while. Thought I'd drop in and see old friends. It's been a long time, Kit. Too long."

He shrugged and glanced at Kelly, his eyes opaque, hiding any feeling he had. "Kelly, this is Althea Kendricks. Allie, Kelly Adams."

The redhead looked at their clasped hands and the slightest frown marred her perfect features. But she recovered quickly.

"How nice to meet you, Kelly," she said smoothly. "Do you live near here?"

"Yes." Kelly was not going to volunteer any information.

Althea flicked another glance at their hands and looked at Kelly. "Maybe you'd like to dance, or something. I can sit with Kit. He and I have a lot to talk about, to catch up on. We were close, did he tell you?"

Kelly looked up in surprised innocence. "No, he never mentioned he was close to another woman. Of course, I know about his wild reputation when he was young, and the groupies that chased him."

Althea drew in a sharp breath, her eyes narrowed at the implied insult. "I didn't chase him! We were engaged."

"That ended years ago, Allie," Kit said, his lips twitching at Kelly's remark. He should have expected Kelly's sassy mouth to come up with something to insult Althea.

"I didn't expect to see you at a dance," Althea said, her eyes running over him.

Kelly turned to look at him, as well. His broad shoulders filled out the Western shirt, and his jeans were new and snug, his boots polished. No one would ever suspect he wasn't still the wild cowboy of his youth. His body was hard, fit, and his legs strong looking. Kelly felt the solid thud of her heart as she assessed him. He was a gorgeous male.

"I came because of Kelly. I didn't want to keep her from the dancing and socializing, but no sense letting the others think they can move in on my claim," he said easily.

The meeting was not going as Althea had wanted, that much was obvious to Kelly. She smiled a broad smile at the older woman and wondered how to get rid of her. While Kit seemed to be handling the confrontation well, she knew he was under a lot of strain. The grip he had on her hand had not eased.

"I'm sure Kelly would like to dance. I'll sit with you." Althea tried once more.

"Kit doesn't need to talk over the old days, Mrs. Kendricks. His best times are now. It was so nice to meet you and see someone from Kit's past. But I'm sure you have other people to visit. Isn't that Annie Carstairs trying to get your attention? Weren't you two in high school together?" Kelly said with false sweetness.

Althea glared at her, then turned back to Kit. "I'll be in town for a while. I'm sure we'll run into each other soon."

Kit chuckled as she walked away and began greeting others at the dance.

"Annie Carstairs is at least seven or eight years older than Althea," he said as he watched her walk away.

"She's well preserved for her age," Kelly said, pulling her aching hand from under his and flexing her fingers.

"She's the same age I am, dammit."

Kelly smiled a teasing grin and cocked her head. "And how old is that, pray?"

"Thirty-three. And it's not old."

"On her it is."

"Meow. What a cat."

Kelly looked as innocent as she knew how. "Excuse me, are you defending her?"

The amusement didn't leave his eyes as he looked at her sitting so close to him. "Not in the least. But you're a little hellcat, insulting her like you did."

"Do you think she caught it?" she asked doubtfully.

He laughed and nodded. "I'm sure. And didn't like it one bit."

"You really wanted to marry her?" Kelly asked, her eyes tracking Althea as she danced in the crowd.

"Yeah. Hard to believe now, isn't it?" His eyes followed her, as well.

"Do you still want her?" Kelly's voice was soft, gentle.

"No. And maybe I'd better make sure she knows it."

He turned to Kelly and slipped his hand up beneath her hair, encircling her neck. Drawing her closer, his mouth closed over hers in a hungry kiss. His lips pressed against hers, moving persuasively until she parted her own and felt the gentle entry of his tongue. She forgot the dance, the townspeople, Althea and their charade as she reveled in the sweet sensations rippling through her at his touch.

His mouth moved and she responded, her whole being caught up with the warm waves of tingling awareness and growing yearning Kit caused. She wished they were alone, and had the whole night ahead of them.

He pulled back a few inches, holding her face close to his, his breath fanning across her cheeks. Kelly stared up at him, unaware of the bemusement in her own expression, her mouth craving his.

"You're still a rowdy cowboy, aren't you?" she asked, her eyes dropping to his lips. "This isn't the place for lovemaking."

"Honey, anywhere I want is the place. And what better spot than where Althea can see it's not her I want, but you."

Four

Kelly started to protest, but Kit simply pulled her against his mouth again and kissed her long and hard.

She was breathing erratically when he released her. "Is that called staking your claim?" she asked, her voice tremulous. Her heart slammed into her chest, blood heating through her body. The other people in the crowded room faded from view. She saw only Kit.

"Yep."

His eyes roamed the room in blatant satisfaction before he looked back at her. "And everyone who needed to know it, saw."

"Oh, great." Embarrassed, she glanced around, noticing people talking, catching the eye of one or two, blushing as she quickly moved hers.

"When Althea leaves, you and I can have a huge fight and everyone will know you're free again," he said softly.

She pulled back and glared at him. "I'm free right now, cowboy. Kisses mean nothing. Don't ride me or I'll walk away and leave you to Althea."

His eyes gleamed. "Don't ride you, when it'd be so much fun?"

Kelly flushed at his words and rose on trembling legs. "I'm going for some food. Want something?" She stepped away from temptation, from danger. She needed a few minutes to get her emotions under control.

"I'll take a plateful."

Kelly kept a watchful eye on Kit as she loaded up two plates with an assortment of the food on the tables. She considered her hasty agreement for the charade. She hadn't thought about it much, just that he'd seemed so upset, and she reacted. His vulnerability struck a chord deep within her. And now that she'd met Althea, she wanted to help him even more. Could they fool the whole town, though? And for how long?

When the dance ended, Clint and Sally offered Kelly a ride home. Accepting, Kelly worried Kit might prove difficult when bidding her good-night. But he didn't say a word. Waving them goodbye, she entered her house wondering at the disappointment that he hadn't at least tried to kiss her again.

Kelly woke late Sunday morning. She was heavy lidded and headachy, wishing for more sleep, knowing her body thought she should be up with the sun. Even after her shower, she was listless. No more late nights for her. After only a couple of weeks in Taylorville she was adjusting to country hours.

There was plenty to do around the house. She could put up shelves so she could unpack her books. She could wash the linens, work on the new storybook. But Sundays were lazy days and she didn't have much motivation. She rather wanted to think about the dance, remember Kit's kisses and the awkward situation with Althea.

She drifted to her backyard, hot in the afternoon sun but shaded by the large oak tree that grew near Molly Benson's yard. She sank into one of the chairs and dozed, lazy and content. San Francisco was probably foggy and cold. She rarely sat out in the afternoons there, unless it was during the warm, sunny days of September.

If she still lived in the city she'd have had brunch with friends, made plans for the week and scarcely had time to do routine chores. Life was slower here, and she was surprised at how fast she was adjusting. Wouldn't her friends be surprised?

"Hi, Kelly. Enjoy the party last night?"

Old Mrs. Benson walked sedately across the yard, two glasses brimful of iced tea on a silver tray. "I brought refreshments." She sat daintily on the second chair and smiled at Kelly.

"Thanks. It sure gets hot." Kelly took a long drink of the icy liquid and settled back, smiling at Mrs. Benson. "The dance was enjoyable. I met a lot of people."

"I saw you sitting with Kit Lockford. He was always a wild boy."

Kelly nodded, but said nothing. Had Molly also seen his kisses? How could she have missed them? Everybody else saw them.

The old woman settled back in her chair and smiled. "I remember how Kit used to come into town, whirling the girls around, buying beer from the store. Then he and his rowdy friends sat on the benches drinking and carrying on. Sassing people as they walked by, flirting with all the girls. Aye, he was a wild one. You'd think nothing could have contained him. All he cared for was being rowdy, having fun and riding the rodeos."

"Rodeos?" Kelly was intrigued. It fit. He was brash and brave and gutsy. He'd have loved the rodeos.

"Yes. That's what he did, ran that ranch of his and rode the rodeo circuit. Rode the broncs and bulls. Won most of the events. When he was away, Clint took care of his ranch."

"The ranch belongs to Kit?" Kelly asked, trying to get it all straight.

"Sure does. Though Clint might be a partner now, for all I know. But it was Kit's. He took over from his mother's brother. Built it up grand with all his winnings. Fixed up that house for Althea. Never thought young Sally Maguire would be its first mistress.''

Kelly was fascinated. ''Kit and Althea were engaged, he told me,'' she said slowly, wondering about them. Did he still want her despite his careless words last night?

''Yes. Wild girl. They made a wonderful couple. She so tall with that rich auburn hair, and as wild as he was. Always egging him on, joining in on the parties, following him to the rodeos.''

''So what happened?'' Kelly knew the result, but not why. She couldn't understand why.

''That young madam tossed him over when she heard the doctor's report that he'd never walk again. Returned his ring while he was still in the hospital. Awful row they had, so I heard. She was screaming at him, and he pleading with her. It ended by her flinging his ring across the room at him as she marched out.''

''God, how awful.'' Kelly's gentle heart ached for the pain he must have gone through, especially just after finding out the extent of his injuries. How cruel of Althea.

''I've always thought so. Kit's not a bad one, just wild. Shameful the way Althea treated him. Though in the long run I think it best Kit learned about her before marriage. I hear her current marriage is breaking up.''

Justice? Kelly wondered.

''The way I heard the story, there was a nurse at the hospital that was hard up, widowed young, had a small child. Kit gave her the ring and told her to sell it and see it brought some happiness somewhere because it sure hadn't brought him any. When he came out, he was a bitter man.''

Kelly couldn't believe Althea had been so cold, so heartless. No wonder he hadn't wanted to appear as if he was still carrying the torch for her. Kelly's anger rose on his behalf as she thought about it.

''Althea married one of the Kendricks boys a few months later. He's in real estate. They live in Stockton. Didn't see him last night. Wouldn't expect to if they are breaking up.''

Kelly didn't want to talk about Althea. She hoped the woman would return to Stockton soon. Maybe she was only in town for the weekend. Had last night fooled her? Kelly fiercely wanted it to have fooled her. She was surprised at the feeling of protectiveness she felt toward Kit. Ha, she'd never met a man who needed less protection.

"How did Kit get hurt?" she asked, curious.

"Rodeoing, like I said. He was at the Cow Palace for the Grand National. Riding a bull. He got gored pretty bad, injured his spine, internal injuries. For a while they didn't know if he'd live."

Kelly shuddered at the picture Molly described. She'd never thought in graphic detail just how he'd become paralyzed.

"The doctors told him he might never walk again, but he's so headstrong he had to prove them wrong. That's why he struggles about on those crutches so much. He's gone a lot farther than anyone thought he would. Though I did hear they wanted him to have another operation. It could improve control beyond what he has. I'm not sure I heard right, though."

"He, uh, he didn't tell me how it happened, just he'd been injured by a bull," Kelly said slowly.

"I don't think he talks about it much. But it festers in him, I think. And I guess he'll never get over it. He keeps himself shut up at that ranch working hard. Doesn't party now. He's changed so much, poor boy."

Kelly smiled gently at Molly Benson. Her words echoed Jefferies from the other day. She understood their sentiments a little better, but Kit Lockford was still too much a man to be called boy. Except for a certain expected bitterness, he'd taken what life had thrown him and continued. Still worked his ranch. And if he didn't socialize, well, after the trauma of his fiancée's defection, he could be excused for avoiding that.

Molly talked at some length about others at the dance and Kelly listened with half an ear, her thoughts caught up with what she'd learned about Kit. She was glad Molly had joined her and filled her in on his background. She had a feeling he'd not be as willing to share. And she didn't want him to know how curious she was about him.

Monday Kelly worked on the story line for her book. She blocked out the chapters, decided what pictures to incorporate for illustrations. And made a schedule of the different stages for completion.

Tuesday she worked at her drawing board in the morning. Taking a break in the early afternoon, she walked down to the store to pick up a few things, and visit with Beth. She saw Jefferies as she was leaving and waved across the street to him, smiling in secret delight. She was beginning to belong. The people in town made her welcome and she felt connected. She had never had that before and it warmed her heart.

Catching a flash of color from the corner of her eye, she turned and watched as Kit Lockford's big blue-and-white truck approached, at a reasonable rate of speed, no less. It slowed and stopped even with her.

Jumping down from the sidewalk, she walked to the driver's door.

"Cop bust you for speeding?" she asked, smiling in delight to see him again. Looking at him almost in hunger, she was startled to realize how glad she was to see him.

"Slowed down just for you, darlin'. Got to keep my best girl happy and she doesn't like speeding in town."

She smiled at his nonsense. "Right, pull the other leg, why don't you?"

"I'll pull them both if you want, and wrap them right around me." He stared down at her for a long moment, while Kelly felt heat rise in her cheeks at the picture his provocative suggestion painted.

He smiled sardonically, as if he could read her mind. "I'm going to Stanton to get some livestock medicine. Want to go for a ride? I want to talk to you."

Kelly considered and nodded. "Why not?"

She went around to the passenger door and climbed in. Excitement welled up inside. She'd never spent very long in his company. It was a half hour's drive to Stanton, the same back. Could they keep from fighting for an hour?

And what did he want to talk about? Had he had second thoughts about their pretending to be involved? Had he decided he wanted to take up again with Althea? She frowned, looking out her window. She didn't want that.

He pulled away, speeding up as the edge of town approached, soon hurtling down the highway. Kelly laughed softly in bravado, knowing he was teasing her.

"I forgot you'd need a special vehicle," she said after a few minutes watching him operate the hand controls. "I didn't know the trucks came with the options."

"I paid a hell of a lot to get this rig. It's four-wheel drive, too, so I can go off-road."

"For ranch work?"

"Right." He didn't say any more and Kelly kept quiet as she watched the rolling brown hills speed by. He might as well be alone in the truck for all the attention he was paying her. She thought he wanted to talk to her. Enough was enough.

"Are you originally from Taylorville?" she asked, just to break the silence.

He threw her a quick look and arched one eyebrow. "Surely the town's busybodies have filled you in on my sordid past by now."

"Do you think all people have to talk about is you?"

He was silent for a minute, then grinned when he heard her.

"Arrogant, self-centered, self-absorbed . . ." She was almost whispering the words, but turned toward him so he'd be sure to hear her.

"Point taken. Yes, I was born at the family ranch about fifteen miles or so north of town."

"And your folks still live there?"

"Sure."

"Other brothers or sisters, besides Clint?"

"No, just the two of us."

"Still nice, for holidays and birthdays and all. You have relatives around."

"Lord, relatives. There's a parcel of them around. I've cousins galore, aunts and uncles. It's downright crowded at holidays, especially Christmas. We all get together at some-one's place and it seems as crowded as the dance the other night."

Kelly smiled, trying to envision it. "When I was little, I always wished for a family, every birthday and every Christmas." She sighed softly and her smile faded. "It never came true."

"A lot of wishes and dreams never come true," he said as they arrived in Stanton.

She glanced at him guiltily. No doubt one day she'd marry and have a family of some sort, so a part of her dream would eventually come true. But what dreams had Kit lost with the loss of his legs? Had he loved Althea? Been dev-astated by her loss? Was he hoping somehow after their charade was played out that he could win her back?

He drove through town and stopped before a large brick building. The sign in front proclaimed Ben Wilson, D.V.M.

"Won't be long." Kit parked the truck in the shade of a large eucalyptus and left his window down. He started up the walk on his crutches and Kelly watched as he swung along the hard-packed dirt. He handled himself well, using his powerful shoulders and arms. His legs looked as if they still had strength in them. Of course, he did have partial use of them. Was it enough to keep them toned?

She wondered how he'd been before. A splendidly fit cowboy riding wild broncs and bulls. She wished she'd known him then, though he wouldn't have looked twice at her. She was not wild and rowdy like Althea. She couldn't have kept up.

It was hot; there was little air stirring. Kelly felt the rivu-lets of water trickle down her back, bead on her forehead, run between her breasts. If he didn't get back soon, she'd melt. She opened the door, searching for a breath of air. The heat from the hot asphalt reflected back.

Just when she was considering following him into the building, which had to be air-conditioned, he came out, a large plastic bag dangling from one hand.

He looked at her when he climbed in, and smiled. "You look like a wilted rag."

She smiled faintly. "I feel like I've just lost ten pounds in body fluids. It's hot!"

"Close to a hundred, I think. How 'bout I buy you an ice cream?"

Kelly smiled. "Sounds great. What did you have to get here?"

"Antiseptic. I've got a couple of steers that tangled badly with barbed wire. I wanted some salve to keep infection at bay. The Frozen Cow is a drive-through. What kind of ice cream do you want?"

In only a short time Kit had procured two tall ice-cream cones. Kelly held his while he drove to a shady spot at the back of the little hut. His hand brushed against hers when he reached for it.

She was already licking hers. The heat was wreaking havoc on the ice cream and it was all she could do to keep it from melting over the edge of the cone.

Kit licked his cone, his eyes watching her. God, she was sexy with that little pink tongue darting here and there to capture errant drips of melting ice cream. He watched as she concentrated on keeping the drips from getting away. When she closed her lips over parts of the frozen confection in an effort to keep ahead of the melt, he felt a hot tightening low down.

He wanted to feel that cold tongue dance with his, have his heat warm her, have his lips press against her cool ones and heat them up. She'd taste of chocolate and woman and her own unique flavor. He couldn't look away. The sensations in his body clamored for release. Clamored for her!

She licked the scoops into a tower shape, and Kit watched fascinated as she took that into her mouth, withdrawing some of it, her lips closed over it as it slowly slid from her heat.

He almost groaned with the desire that swept through him. He had it badly if he thought eating an ice cream was erotic. But all he could think of when she moved her tongue and mouth was how it would feel against him. If she would lick him like that tower in her cone, if she would put her mouth...

He threw his ice cream from the window, heard it land with a soft plop on the grassy verge.

"What's wrong?" Kelly asked, surprise in her voice.

"Nothing." Nothing he could tell her, for God's sake. "I didn't want it after all." He kept his eyes straight ahead. His hands reached for the steering wheel and he held it in a tight grip. He hadn't felt like this in over two years. With a sense of shock he realized he'd thought he'd never feel like this again. Not after the accident. Not after what Althea had made perfectly clear.

But he did. He wanted Kelly Adams in the most primitive, carnal way. He wanted to feel her hands against his skin, her hot mouth on him, her tongue mating with his, then moving against his skin. He wanted the same erotic licking on his skin she was doing with that damned ice cream.

He closed his eyes in frustration. Wouldn't she laugh if she ever suspected! Or would she be embarrassed and try to say something to let him down easily? She was kind. Her help at the dance showed him that. He sighed.

"What did you want to talk to me about?" she asked, her teeth crunching into the crisp cone. He turned back, watching her nibble at the cone, his jeans so tight he was in pain. He shifted slightly away from her, praying she wouldn't notice his arousal. Two years ago he'd have made some smart remark and drawn her attention to how she made him feel. Not now. Why, a girl like Kelly could have anybody. The last thing she'd want was a cripple making a play for her.

He gazed at the shrubs and trees that offered scant shade, desperately trying to ignore her tongue's forays on the ice cream.

"I called Will Smith about the black pony. He told me where he's grazing. If you want to go see him, I can take you tomorrow."

"Great, I sure would. Thanks a lot. I have the sketches I did of Popo, but the expression on the black pony's face seemed so sad. I'd love to see him up close."

Was that the writer in her, seeing an expression on a pony's face? Damn, it was just a black pony. Probably bored to tears waiting for the Smiths' grandbaby to grow up. But instead of disgust at her sentimentality, Kit found himself hoping the damned pony still looked sad tomorrow so she wouldn't be disappointed.

"What time can we go?"

"I'll pick you up late morning," he said, wondering now if it was a good idea. He'd be smarter to stay as far from her as he could. He couldn't afford to get tangled up with any woman. Althea had put his heart through a wringer. He couldn't risk that happening a second time. And just being around Kelly had him more aware of her subtle femininity than anyone in the past dozen years.

"Can we have a picnic? I'll bring the food?" she asked, finishing the last of her cone and wiping her hands and mouth on her napkin.

Kit turned his head to watch her, unable to help himself. Holding the wheel tightly so he didn't reach over to grab her, he watched as the napkin wiped off the lingering traces of ice cream. He'd like to lick the stickiness from around her lips, feel the softness of her skin against him. Then plunge into her cool mouth and heat it with the fire that raged through him. She was driving him crazy and she didn't even have a clue.

"Yeah, we can have a picnic." He started the truck and backed out to the street. The ride home was as silent as the ride to Stanton had been. Kelly wondered why he'd invited her along. He hadn't said much to her and he could have told her about the pony while they were in front of Beth's store.

Kelly didn't understand the silence. But even more she didn't understand the rising tension in the cab. She was aware of him as she'd never been aware of a man before—his long legs not far from her on the bench, his broad shoulders and strong arms and hands. What would it be like to have those hands on her? He'd never touched her, except to hold her hand so tightly last Saturday it had ached for two days. And kiss her. The memory of his kiss in her hallway flashed through her, the way his body had leaned against hers, the heat of his muscles, the hard ridge of his arousal. Had he wanted more than a kiss? How could she let him know she might want more herself?

Her face flamed and she stuck her hand out the window to divert some of the rushing air into the cab, to cool her down. If possible. The air was as hot as she was. Would he kiss her again? Or was that only for show, to prove something to Althea Kendricks?

"Did Althea leave yet?" she asked as they drew near Taylorville. She was glad she was almost home. What if she did something stupid? Like run her hand down his thigh, brush her fingers through the small openings between the buttons of his shirt, knock his hat off to feel his thick hair?

"No." The word was short, harsh.

"Oh." Had he seen her again since the dance? She clenched her hands into fists.

"She called Sally. Don't ask me why, she's years older than Sally and they were never friends. But she's staying in town for a while, at her folks'."

She studied him as he drove. His lips were drawn into a thin line and his eyes narrowed. Was it from the glare of the sun, or in anger at Althea? He must know she'd called Sally to let him know she was staying. What was Althea doing? Had Althea decided Kit was the man for her after all and come back to get him?

"So we continue pretending?" Kelly asked hesitantly. Or had Saturday night been enough to salvage his pride?

He flicked her a quick glance and nodded. "We continue."

She smiled and settled back on the seat, quietly satisfied. The situation was dangerous. She was already far more interested in this cowboy than she should be. She felt protective toward him and he didn't need it. She felt indignant on his behalf at the way Althea had behaved. And she ached for the freedom and way of life he'd lost with the accident.

But there was nothing to pity in the man. There was excitement, enchantment and exhilaration being with him. And danger. Danger to her heart and her own peace of mind. Kelly tried never to kid herself. It hadn't worked as a child, it wouldn't work as an adult. She could help Kit out. But that was as far as it would go. No matter how much she might wish for more.

"Why did you agree to help me, Kelly?" he asked softly.

She stared at him, not wanting to confess the real reason. She carefully thought out her words. "Well, I guess as a lark." She would never have considered herself a femme fatale, someone to score off another woman. That held immense appeal. "And I guess because I don't like to be beholden to anyone. You're going to take me to see the black pony. If I can help you out, we'll be sort of even."

He nodded at her words but didn't respond. Devastation seared him. *As a lark.* Damn, Althea had been right. Women wouldn't want anything to do with a scarred cripple. Kelly was helping him out as a lark, just for fun. When Althea left, Kelly would forget him as fast as they'd met.

He pulled in to her driveway and stopped.

"Thanks for the ride and the ice cream," she said, putting her hand on his arm.

"Any time," he said, feeling her touch pierce straight through to his heart. He wanted to pull her into his arms, make the day's heat fade in contrast to the fire roiling through him. But he didn't even look at her. It was safer not to.

"I'll be by in the morning."

She hesitated a moment then jerked her hand free. Opening her door, she slid across the seat and out into the hot afternoon sun.

"Do you like anything special for lunch?" she asked, slamming the door and looking in through the window, anger simmering in her tone.

He looked at her then. It was safe; he couldn't reach her. But why the spurt of temper? Her eyes were icy as they glared back at him. For a moment he wondered if she had wanted him to kiss her. It hit him hard in the gut.

"Anything you fix will be fine." *Anything you do will be fine,* he thought, unable to look away from the icy disdain in her blue eyes.

"All I can say is you don't seem like a wild hellion to me. I think you're nothing but a...but a...but a pussycat!" Turning, Kelly marched up her driveway and around to the back of her house, head held high, back rigid and straight.

Kit stared after her in amazement, his eyes tracking her until she disappeared from view. *A pussycat?* Goddammit! For two cents he'd go after her and make her eat her words.

His hand on the door handle, he paused. The gleam in his eyes was sudden. He'd wait. Tomorrow he'd have her alone, out on the Smiths' ranch, totally at his mercy. Then he'd show her what a pussycat he was.

Five

The next morning promised to be as hot as the previous one. Kelly dressed in a loose yellow top and white shorts. In deference to any walking they might do at the Smiths' ranch, she wore socks and tennis shoes, instead of sandals. Her feet were hot before she finished tying the laces. She drew her hair back into a high ponytail to keep it off her neck.

Preparing the picnic lunch, Kelly hoped she had things he'd like, wishing she had a basket. Stuffing everything into a paper bag and a cooler, she located an old blanket, got her sketch pad and stacked everything on the front porch. She didn't know when he'd arrive, but she was ready.

Kelly was surprised at the surge of delight that swept through her when Kit drove up. She had a hard time keeping the smile from splitting her face as she gathered her things and walked slowly to the truck. No sense letting him know how glad she was to see him. She was sure the feeling wasn't mutual. She still wondered why he'd offered to take her to see the pony.

"Good morning," she said gaily, peering into the cab.

"Put the things in the back and let's go."

She complied, quickly opening the passenger door and climbing in.

"Don't you ever use normal social amenities like good morning, how are you, nice to see you?" she asked as she fastened her seat belt.

"Why?" He threw the truck into reverse and backed quickly to the highway, then accelerated.

"It's a polite way to greet people when you haven't seen them in a while."

"I saw you yesterday."

"That's a while." A long while if you were counting minutes until he was back.

"If I wanted to chat up some woman, I might try it. Otherwise, why bother? You see me. What does *hi* accomplish."

She shrugged, no longer willing to argue about something so unimportant. She was going to enjoy today, no matter how obnoxious Kit Lockford became. She could handle him. She'd had a long talk with herself last night and was ready to deal with the man today. She hoped.

She watched as the familiar scenery rushed by. She'd driven this road a couple of times when first exploring the area. The hills rose and fell with regularity, deserted and barren except for the drying grass and enclosing barbed-wire fences. Here and there a clump of trees offered relief from the monotonous scenery. The sky was cloudless, pale blue and brassy. The sun was already hot, and the worst heat of the day was still ahead.

Kit turned onto a dirt trail barred by a metal gate.

"Open it, wait for me to drive through, then close it behind us," he said as he stopped.

"Can we go there?"

"Sure, as long as we close the gate behind us."

She jumped down from the high cab and quickly unlatched the metal gate. It was lightweight, easy to move as she swung it wide so the truck could pass. Closing it behind them, she double-checked the latch to make sure it was fastened. Then she got back in the truck.

"Fasten your seat belt tight. It'll get bumpy from here and I don't want you to hit your head," Kit instructed.

Kelly glanced at him. He probably didn't want her head to dent the roof of his truck. She doubted he had any concerns for her safety. Yet as she complied, she noticed he'd already fastened his own belt.

They followed the dirt road for a while then Kit swung left, put his drive train into four-wheel and began climbing one of the low hills. The truck lurched and bounced as it traversed the natural terrain, spinning up dirt, leaving a trailing plume of dust behind.

Reaching the summit of the small hill, Kit paused and looked around. In the distance, to the right, a small grove of live oaks rose from the grassy hill. Beneath the trees, near the edge of sunlight, stood the black pony.

They reached the trees in only minutes, Kit taking care to cover the last quarter mile slowly and easily so as not to spook the pony.

His brown eyes watching curiously, the pony stood his ground as the truck approached. Kelly held her breath, afraid he'd turn and run away. But his ears pricked forward, his nostrils flared slightly, as he watched. He didn't seem afraid, only curious.

Kit stopped, turned off the engine. Silence swept through the cab. There was only the heat rising from the ground, from the engine cover, shimmering in waves. Otherwise there was silence. Silence as Kelly had never heard before. She could hear her own breathing. Hear Kit's.

"We'll sit beneath the trees. It'll be cooler there."

"Okay." She opened the door, her eyes still on the pony. He ambled closer, curious. Smiling in delight, she stretched out a hand. As he drew nearer, she reached out and tentatively stroked his soft, hot neck, the black hair drawing the heat from the sun.

"There's a small brown bag in the back. Get it," Kit called. He hadn't moved, just sat watching her.

"What's in it?" She turned to do as he'd asked.

"Carrots and apples. I thought the little guy would like a treat."

She smiled as her heart almost exploded in tenderness at his thoughtfulness. What a complex man Kit Lockford was. Arrogant, bossy and bad tempered, yet kind enough to remember to bring a treat for a pony.

She grabbed the bag and opened it, taking out a carrot. Holding it away from her as if it might bite, or as if the pony would bite her, she approached him gingerly.

Kit chuckled. "He won't bite you. Let him take a bite or two, then put the rest on your open palm. He'll take it nicely."

Kelly wasn't too sure of that. The first crunch startled her and she dropped the carrot. The pony nuzzled her hand, then dropped his head to forage on the grass, finding and finishing the carrot.

Kit slid across the seat, out of the truck, balanced on his crutches. He moved beside Kelly and took her hand in his, taking another carrot from the bag. When the pony approached, Kelly tried to shrink back, but Kit's bulk was behind her, solid and unmoving. His hand held hers firmly as she offered the treat.

When the pony daintily bit off two chunks, Kit turned her hand, opening and placing the remaining carrot flat. "Now hold still."

Soft velvety lips brushed over her palm and seized the carrot. Crunching placidly, he finished it.

She smiled in delight. "That was great!" She turned and found herself against Kit, his arm still half around her, balanced on his crutches. Her smile faded as she met the look in his eyes. She was caught, couldn't move, couldn't look away. Could only look deep into his dark blue eyes and feel herself captivated as she'd never been before. Her breathing became constricted and she felt dizzy, disoriented. Taking a deep breath, she knew it had been a mistake. She smelled the drying grass, the pony and the hot, masculine scent of Kit Lockford.

The pony butted her in the back, searching for more treats. Kelly lost her balance and crashed into Kit, her soft breasts pressed against his hard chest, her legs brushing against the soft denim of his jeans. He lost his balance and fell back against the side of the truck. Both remained upright, though his arms dropped the crutches to enclose Kelly and keep her from falling.

"Oh, I'm sorry," she said against his shoulder, her head naturally finding a comfortable spot. "Are you okay?"

She pushed back, but he wouldn't let her go. She could feel the muscles of his chest bunch beneath her, his legs long and hard. As she moved to find her balance, her hips brushed against him and she froze a second, feeling the unmistakable sign this man wanted her.

She pushed back, meeting his amused eyes. Flustered and embarrassed and a little aroused herself, she tried to stand, brushing against him again, her breasts tingling with desire as waves of realization rippled through her. Her hands clutched his shoulders and she had to stop herself from tracing the muscles she could feel beneath her fingers. She tried to push away from the solid wall of his chest, but the proximity drained her strength. It was a fight to move away.

"I'm okay," she said breathlessly.

"I'm not," he said, and lowered his head to her parted lips.

Kelly closed her eyes against the bright sky and gave herself up to the pleasure of his kiss. His lips moved against hers, his tongue traced the seam of hers, before sliding through to explore the soft inner reaches of her mouth.

His hands held her loosely, his mouth doing all the work, driving her crazy with longings and desire. She met his thrusting tongue with her own, tasting his own special sweetness, following back to his mouth. She pressed closer, responding avidly to the sensations and enchantment his touch delivered.

Giving up the fight to part, she let her hands move across his shoulders, to the strong column of his neck, feeling the heat of his skin, the soft hair that brushed against her fingers as she reached up to encircle him.

Another nudge from the pony broke the kiss.

"Hey, go find your own girl," Kit protested, trying to protect Kelly from the curiosity of the pony.

She giggled slightly and reluctantly pulled back, embarrassed by the instant response she'd given. Turning to pick up the bag of treats from where she'd dropped it on the ground, her shaky fingers withdrew a piece of fruit.

"Here's an apple." She held it out gingerly, her fingers dancing around the edge as the pony bit into it.

"You're a pushy little thing," she said as he butted her chest with his forehead, his soft lips nibbling around her hand.

"Sam." Kit still leaned against the truck, watching them, his expression relaxed.

"What?" She looked at him.

"His name's Sam."

"That's not a very pony name." She looked back at the little pony. He had apparently figured out there were no more treats and was calmly grazing on some of the drying grass.

Kit chuckled, his arms crossed across his chest.

"What's a pony name?"

Kelly thought for a moment that that was what he had looked like before the accident. His eyes were amused, his look superior and arrogant, like the supremely self-confident man he was. To look at him she couldn't tell he was unable to walk unaided. He looked virile, muscular and potent. Too potent for her.

She casually reached down and picked up his crutches, handing them to him without a word, and without a look of sympathy.

"I don't know. Popo's not bad. Trigger, maybe, or Silver? But not Sam."

He took the crutches, his eyes on her, tension now evident in his face. His concentration seemed to be on how she was treating him.

"Sam's as good as any."

"He still looks sad," she said. She refused to let him dwell on his limitations, or make her dwell on them.

"He looks like a pony." Kit scowled and pushed away from the truck, moving over the broken ground toward the shade.

"What did you bring for lunch?" he asked.

She closed the door and reached into the back of the truck for the picnic she'd brought. Carting everything to the shade beneath the old trees, she dropped the bag and cooler and spread the blanket out on the most level spot she could find.

Kit stood at the blanket's edge for a long time, considering how to get down. Damnation. He shouldn't have brought her. Should never have agreed to a picnic. First there was the problem of getting down. Then how would he get back up?

He turned away, considering the distance back to the truck. Maybe he'd just sit in there and forget . . .

"Are you scouting for Indians, or are you going to sit down here and eat?" she asked as she began drawing things from the brown bag. She spread a small tablecloth in the center of the blanket and drew out the sandwiches she'd made earlier. Opening the cooler, she withdrew the mayonnaise. She just had to coat the bread, and the sandwiches would be ready to eat.

"I'm not sure I can," Kit said, looking down at her.

Kelly understood instantly.

She stood slowly, brushing the crumbs from her fingertips and walking over to Kit. He was so tall standing there proudly, anger and bitterness shining from his face. It must be awful.

She stood up to him and met his gaze straight on.

"I'm only going to say this once."

"I don't want pity," he snapped.

She looked surprised, then nodded. "Okay. Try this on. Why did you bring me here?"

He stared down at her, unable to tell her he wanted to be with her, spend time with her alone. For a moment he for-

got where they were. He could lose himself in those sparkling eyes of hers. Her silky white-blond hair tantalized him,
enticed him to tangle his rough hands in it, comb the silky
softness through his fingers. Her long brown legs tempted
him in a different manner and it was all he could do to keep
from saying it to her.

"You wanted to see the pony," he said at last.

"Yes, I did. Why did you bring me?"

"Who else would?"

"Why did you?" she persisted.

"Dammit, I don't know. I knew you wanted to use him
in your story and thought you'd like to see him close up. I
was just trying to help."

She smiled as if he'd just won first prize at the county fair.
"Help me, huh?"

"Kelly, it isn't—"

"Kit Lockford, did you help me because you pity me?"
She'd make a fine actress, he thought, studying her stricken
look. Only the dancing lights in her eyes betrayed her.

"Dammit, Kelly, it's not—"

"Did you!" She pushed a sharp index finger against his
chest, forcing him to answer her.

"No, of course not."

"Then I can help you sit down and get up and we'll get
this picnic on the road." She tilted her head and stared at
him as if daring him to defy what she'd said.

"I can get down all right. I can always just fall. It's getting back up I don't think I can do. And I'm too heavy for
you to lift."

Her finger softened and two others joined it as she slid
them between the gaps of his buttons. Lightly she stroked
the heated skin of his chest, just an inch or two, but Kit felt
as if his whole body was on fire for her.

"I'm very strong," she said softly, her eyes like liquid
pools of deep blue water. Her voice a whisper, like the wind
through the treetops on a summer day. He sighed. He was
lost and he knew it. But he wouldn't let her know.

"All right. If you have to drive out by yourself and get Clint, it'll serve you right," he said, moving to the edge of the blanket.

Kelly thought he moved gracefully as he sank onto the blanket. He had some strength in his left leg, and used that to get down. She fixed the lunch and they ate companionably watching the pony graze, staring out over the rolling grasslands.

When they'd finished, he leaned back on his elbows to watch as Kelly drew out her sketch pad and began bringing the pony to life on the pages beneath her fingers. It was hot, dry and still. She was glad she'd brought so much soda. They'd both finished one with lunch and she already had a second.

"How come you never came to visit Margaret while she was alive?" he asked after a long time.

"I didn't know about her," she replied, filling in some of the background around the pony. Flipping to a clean sheet, she tried to capture the pony taking the apple.

"What do you mean? She left her house to you, didn't she? How could you not know her?"

"Actually, she left her house to my mother, or her issue. My mother died years ago, so according to the attorneys, I got it through her. She was Aunt Margaret's only niece."

Kelly put the pad down and turned a bit so she could see Kit as she talked to him. See exactly what his reactions were when she told him about herself. So far Molly Benson was the only one she'd told about her family. How would Kit feel?

"My mother wasn't married to my father. Her family cast her off before I was born. As far as I know, there was never any attempt made to heal the breach. That much I learned from the attorney when he located me. My mother died before I was four."

"Four? Where did you live?"

"An assortment of foster homes in and around San Francisco. The longest one was for three years. But then they got transferred and I was assigned to a different one."

She tried to keep the bleakness from her voice. She didn't want Kit's pity about her childhood any more than he wanted pity because of his physical limitations. But she could see from his look she'd not been successful.

He didn't say anything for a long moment. When he did speak, he surprised her. "So that's why you thought a large family was so special?" He'd remembered what she'd said.

She nodded. "One day I want to get married and have about fifteen children. I want to have a family around me, and . . . and feel like I belong somewhere." She'd never told anyone else about her desire to belong somewhere. Would he think she was foolish wishing to belong?

He nodded. "I can understand that. I've belonged here forever. I can't even imagine what it would have been like not to have both parents, all my aunts, uncles, grandparents. Cousins." He frowned. "Though I could use a few less cousins. You want some of mine?"

She smiled gently and shook her head. "I'll wait for my family, the one my husband's sure to have."

Kit looked away at that, an old familiar ache building in his chest. One day she'd find some man who would light up her face. She'd marry him and he'd kiss those soft lips, taste her skin, bring her to passion and ecstasy. And give her all the children she wanted. But it wouldn't be him.

He lay back and tilted his hat over his head. He didn't want to talk anymore. He didn't want to think about how soft she felt against him when he kissed her. How her kisses awakened his senses to a fever pitch he never remembered from before. And he sure as hell didn't want to think about another man having the right to love Kelly, live with her, when he would still be alone.

Kelly watched for a moment, but Kit seemed to be going to sleep. She turned back to the pony and continued to draw him, studying how he was made, how he moved as he slowly walked along cropping the grass.

Flipping to a new page, Kelly shifted slightly on the blanket and smiled. Her pencil flew, sketching Kit sleeping, like an old-time cowboy, hat tilted to cover his face, long legs stretched out, crossed at the ankles. The dusty boots and hat were hard to capture. She did another sketch, this one from memory, of Kit leaning against the truck, arms crossed over his chest. She flushed slightly as she sketched over his jeans. Maybe she wouldn't be as accurate as she ought.

She studied the picture, pleased to see she'd captured the freedom and pride of her cowboy. Sighing gently, she closed the sketchbook and laid it beside her.

She looked over at Kit, wondering how long ago he had been injured. She moved the picnic things to the edge of the blanket and lay down near him, propping her head up on one hand, watching him. For a long moment Kelly tried to envision him as Molly had described him—wild, rowdy, fun loving. He was devilishly attractive, tall, sexy, virile. Kelly had no doubt he'd have set many hearts tripping faster when he rode into town.

For that matter, even now when he looked at her, her own heart began tripping faster. He was one sexy man. Did he know, she wondered?

Gently she pushed his hat away from his face, toppled it to the blanket on the far side.

Kit opened one eye a slit and looked at her.

"This is a fine picnic," Kelly said softly, her finger daringly tracing his eyebrow, down his cheek, tracing the strong line of his jaw. "My subject wanders away and my companion falls asleep."

"Didn't you realize you were that boring?" he asked lazily, capturing her hand in his, squeezing slightly.

"I am not boring!" she said indignantly.

He chuckled at her tone and rolled over on his side facing her. "No, that's true, Kelly, you are anything but boring."

He threaded his hand into the soft swirls of her hair, loosening the ponytail. He drew her face to his, his eyes watching her as he slowly moved her closer. She stared back, unafraid, unresisting. Twice her glance flicked to his lips and he almost felt as if she'd touched him. Finally her lids began to drift closed as he brought her to him.

His mouth was soft and tender as he nibbled against her lips, teasing for a response. When she inched closer and relaxed her lips, he parted them and plunged into the sweet darkness of her mouth.

Kelly moved closer, wanting his kiss to go on forever. His tongue inflamed her, excited her, built desire within to a fever pitch. His lips were magic against hers, drawing a deeper response than she'd ever known before. She moved to give him as much pleasure as he was giving her.

His hand moved slowly from her head, gently down her neck to her shoulder. Her hands reached for him, feeling the heat from his chest through the thin cotton of his shirt. Slowly she moved to the buttons, slipping them through the holes, wanting to feel his bare skin against her fingertips.

His hand moved down to the hem of her shirt, and slowly slipped beneath with feathery touches against her heated skin as his mouth continued its sweet assault. Kelly shivered in delight and paused in her own seeking as new sensations flooded through her, heat and fire and light and confusion, the wild delight of his touch awaking a long-dormant need deep inside.

His hand moved against her skin, the roughness of his hardened palms tracing gently over her silky skin. When he reached her unbound breasts she froze, suspended in anticipation, desire hot and fevered pulsing through her.

She trembled, her hand gripping the material of his shirt as she waited endless moments for his hand to touch her where she most wanted. His thumb brushed the soft underside of her breast. Kelly ached for more. She moaned softly in the back of her throat, shifting to let him know she wanted more.

Kit pulled back, breaking their kiss to gaze down at her as she slowly lifted her lids. He could see the blatant desire she couldn't conceal.

"Don't stop," she whispered, afraid he'd draw back, the moistness between her legs crying for attention, her breasts aching for his touch, her whole body aching for completion.

"I wasn't planning to," he said equally softly, his hand moving to engulf her breast, squeeze gently as his thumb brushed across her nipple, feeling the rigid tip, watching as the sexual pleasure flashed in her eyes. She moaned again and moved restlessly, wanting more, much more.

"Do you like that?" he asked, keenly aware of her delight and pleasure. His thumb feathered across her again.

"Do it harder," she whispered, twisting and moving her hips in agitation.

Kit pushed her shirt up, exposing both breasts to his gaze, one still captured with his hand.

"God, Kelly, you're beautiful."

"Don't stop," she breathed again, rolling to her back, offering herself up to him, her hand tugging his shirt so that he moved with her.

His hot mouth covered the firm nub and took her into a cavern of delight. He suckled against her skin, laving the tip of her nipple with his raspy tongue as waves of shimmering ecstasy coursed through Kelly. His hand moved against the soft satin of her skin, lower as he traced the dip of her navel, pressing against her as she moved her hips.

Kelly's hands pushed at Kit's shirt, releasing the last button as she pulled it from his jeans, her hands moving against his skin, learning his shape, feeling his warmth burn her hotter than the sun.

When he raised his head, she clutched at him. But he only moved to capture the other nipple and give equal treatment.

Kelly was on fire. The waves of pleasure were swamping her and she moved rhythmically seeking fulfillment, completion, satisfaction. Her hands clutched his shoulders as his hand slipped beneath the elastic waist of her shorts, seeking the heat, the dark center of her. She strained against him, pushing the shirt from his shoulders, her hands sliding over his sweat-slicked back.

"Kit." She urged him on, her hands now seeking the waistband of his jeans.

"Shh, easy, sweetheart, easy. I don't have any protection for you. Just enjoy, Kelly. Enjoy," he said against her skin, his tongue flicking against her throbbing breast, his hand finding her center and pressing against the dampness he found.

She was hot and moist and seeking relief. Slowly, slowly he moved his hand, feeling the heat, aching to possess her, to come to completion himself. But he couldn't. Damn, he'd never expected to come this far, not once during the past two years. She was driving him crazy with wanting, yet he couldn't have her.

His tongue thrust in and out to match the tempo of his hand, to match the tempo of her undulating hips. His voice, low, hoarse, ragged, urged her toward the summit of her satisfaction. He felt her straining against him. Her breasts brushed his chest and he lay halfway across her, the soft mounds crying for his attention, but he couldn't leave her sweet mouth.

Her hands gripped his shoulders and he raised his head, looking at her, watching her spiral toward ecstasy.

Her eyes flew open just as he felt her tighten convulsively. Pulsating, throbbing, she raised her hips, her eyes wide and glazed.

"Come on, honey. Let go."

"Kit!" She chanted his name over and over and over as waves of rapture rippled through her. Her hands clenched against him, pulling him closer, wanting all of him.

God, he *hurt!* He wanted to plunge into that welcoming sheath and feel her convulse around him. But he couldn't. Not today. Taking what he could get, he lowered his mouth to hers again, plunging into her sweetness, reveling in the hot response she gave.

Gradually she quieted. It was so hot. She felt as if she had melted and been reborn. His mouth was gently nibbling her lips now, moving to her cheeks, her nose, back to her lips. But his wonderful magical fingers were still. Soon he'd pull away and she'd be alone again, but for now, she wanted to imprint everything on her mind so she could always remember.

Her arms were heavy, she was so hot. Slowly her hands relaxed their grip, soothed the strong shoulder muscles, drew lazy circles against his burning skin.

He pulled back and looked down at her. She opened her eyes slightly, so tired and satiated she could scarcely move. Her arms fell to the blanket. Her legs were still spread, his hand a hot brand against her femininity. Her eyes watched him watch her as he drew slowly back from her. She sighed and moved to snuggle closer, closing her legs against his hand, not wanting him to leave her.

He chuckled and brought his hand from her shorts, and lay back, pulling her across his chest. Kelly's head lay on his shoulder, and her arm went to cross his chest. She was as relaxed as she'd ever been. The rapid pounding of his heart beneath her ear showed her he had been affected, as well.

"I'm so tired," she said.

"Then go to sleep." His voice was soft against her ear.

"Umm."

He thought she had fallen asleep when she caressed his chest and mumbled.

"Next time bring protection."

Six

He held the armful of soft femininity against his chest, knowing instantly when she fell asleep by her total relaxation. Trusting him. God, she smelled so good, felt so good, and it had been so long. He closed his eyes as his hand pushed her shirt out of the way and gently rubbed her soft skin. It was like the softest silk. All over. He wondered if the calluses on his fingers and palms were rough on her. She was incredibly soft. And sweet.

And he'd never hurt with wanting anyone so much in his life.

But there would be no next time. Another time she'd want to have his shirt off, not just open. To make love to her he'd have to shuck his jeans. And once she saw the scars, the ridges and puckered skin where the bull had gored and the doctors had patched, she would be so disgusted she wouldn't want anything further to do with him.

He hadn't wanted a woman in the past two years. He hadn't known before meeting Kelly that he'd ever want a woman again. But just being around her kept him in a partial state of arousal. After today, he'd have to keep his distance. He couldn't stand for another woman to rail at him as Althea had. He couldn't bear to have Kelly disgusted with his scars.

But he'd have today to remember. She had been so responsive, so passionate. God, he wished he could have had her!

His fingers gentled in her hair, brushing it back from her flushed face. She was hot. The sheen of perspiration made her skin glow. She was so pretty. What was she doing out here with him? Was this a lark, too?

He eased her yellow top down over her, raising her a little to bring it between them, covering her, tingling awareness still shimmering between them. He wished he could hold her forever. Gradually she cooled down. Gradually he did, too, but the ache didn't go away.

Kelly woke slowly, conscious first of the slow, steady heartbeat beneath her ear. Taking a breath, she inhaled Kit's scent. He smelled of sunshine and grass, of tangy after-shave and masculine power, his scent uniquely his own. Lying still, she breathed steadily, smiling in sensual satisfaction.

Slowly she flexed her fingers against his chest, pulling the crisp hair slightly, rubbing against the rock-hard muscles clearly defined beneath his warm skin.

"Awake?" he mumbled softly, his eyes still closed as he held her.

"Mmm-hmm. Was I asleep long?"

"Don't know. I fell asleep, too. You ready to go?"

"Not just yet." Kelly was caught in an awkward situation she didn't know how to handle. She'd gone to bed with only one other man—boy, actually—when she'd been in college and wanted to see what all the talk was about. They'd gone steady for weeks before. But she hardly knew Kit. How did she face him now? What was the proper after-love etiquette? If anyone knew it, it had to be this wild cowboy.

Idly her hand moved against him, relishing the feel of his skin beneath her fingertips, the crisp curly hair on his chest, the hard muscles of his stomach. The coarse ridges...

Kelly went still, her fingertips tracing scar tissue across his abdomen, around his waist to his back. Disappearing beneath the waistband of his jeans.

Kit caught her hand and dragged it away.

"Don't," he said, his voice hard.

"Did it hurt?" she asked, raising her head to look at him.

"It hurt like hell at the time. Doesn't now. Let's go." He eased her away, drawing his shirt together in front and sitting up, turning away from her.

Kelly sat up, knelt, sank on her ankles, puzzled. What was wrong?

"Kit, I know you must have scars from the accident. But they don't matter. I have a scar from appendicitis."

"Dammit, Kelly, these don't compare to some slight scar a doctor did below your bikini line. We're talking revulsive enough to turn a strong woman's stomach."

She stared at him in disbelief, in growing horror. Had those been Althea's words to him in hospital? God, no wonder he wanted nothing to do with her.

She scooted around to face him, rising up on her knees to be higher than he was. Her hands reached out and jerked his shirt, her blue eyes blazing down into his.

"Now just a damn minute, Kit Lockford. Don't you go telling me what will turn my stomach, because you don't know me at all. Are you so caught up in perfection that a slight imperfection is cause to reject a person?"

"Of course not. But—"

"But nothing, cowboy. Let me see." She tugged at his shirt, popping two buttons he'd already fastened. He pulled the shirt closed, trying to fend her off, but she jerked up the edge and stared at the lines that crisscrossed his skin.

Lightly she traced them. His muscles jerked beneath her touch.

Mischievously she grinned up at him. "Are you ticklish?"

"No." But the way he said it, she knew.

She ran her fingers over his side and he squirmed away, laughing. "Stop it."

She laughed and leaned closer, her hands on his shoulders. Her smile faded and she leaned even closer.

"You better hope I have a strong stomach or you're going to have a mess all over you." She closed the distance to his lips and kissed him hard.

Pulling away before he could reach for her, she snapped up to her feet, straightening her shorts, pulling her sadly wrinkled shirt down, trying to stretch out some of the wrinkles.

"They are not so bad," she said, catching his gaze.

"The worst are lower," he said, buttoning his shirt, searching around for his hat.

He refused to meet her eye and Kelly wondered at the awful words he had said. Her heart ached for him.

"What do you do with your other women, make love in the dark? Only let them touch your shoulders?" she asked as she went to get the bag and cooler to load in the back of the truck. She tucked her pad into the brown bag.

"There are no other women," he said shortly.

She looked at him. "Since when?"

"Since the accident."

"How long ago?"

"Over two years."

She stared in disbelief. This gorgeous hunk of man was telling her he had not made love in over two years? What was wrong with the women in Tuolumne County? What was wrong with him?

"Why not?" She sank down, her legs refusing to hold her.

"Why the hell do you think? I told you the worst ones are lower."

"I can't wait for you to show them to me," she said.

"Hell, Kelly, I'm not such a masochist that I'll set myself up for something like that. There won't be another time."

She saw the determination in his eyes, but was too stunned to argue. Slowly she gathered the things and put them in the truck.

Going back, she knew she still had to help him rise. Would he let her?

He had his crutches beside him, his left leg bent, boot firmly planted on the ground.

"What do you want me to do?" she asked, avoiding his glance lest he see the hurt she was feeling.

"Let's try it with you behind me. If I can get enough leverage to get up on the crutch handles, I can make it up the rest of the way."

She went behind him and waited until he had the crutches beside him. Then she reached beneath his arms, and straightened. He came up as easily as if one leg wasn't totally useless. She held him for a brief second before stepping back. Leaning over, she folded the blanket, keeping her face averted.

"Thanks." The word was forced out. She could hear the strain and bitterness behind it.

"Sure." She went to the truck, tossed the blanket in back and climbed in, almost burning her legs on the hot seat. She carefully fastened her seat belt. Even with the windows open, the cab felt like an oven.

When Kit got in, his face was shuttered, closed. He didn't say anything, just started the truck and slammed it into gear.

The ride home was long and tension filled. Kelly resolutely stared out of her side window, her lips tightly closed against the pain now growing in her heart. She knew the rodeo accident had been awful, traumatic, changing the entire course of his life. But in two years he should be more reconciled. Especially to the scars.

Her fingers tingled in her lap as if they remembered the feel of his hot skin, the strength of his muscles, the wiry hair on his chest. Her breasts ached to feel his touch again, to feel his mouth opened on her, his hands moving against her, the solid wall of his chest.

She took a deep, shaky breath. She couldn't keep thinking about it. She'd go mad. Especially if he didn't want her anymore.

Tears filled her eyes at the thought, but she resolutely blinked them away, willing him to drive as fast as he normally did, willing the journey to be finished soon. Before she broke down and cried.

Finally he turned in to her driveway.

She reached for the handle, but his hand caught her arm and held her in her seat. She turned to look at him.

"Are you all right?" He hadn't planned to ask her that, but the look on her face stopped the words he'd been going to say.

She nodded.

"I didn't hurt you?"

She shook her head. He was hurting her, but not the way he meant.

She dropped her gaze to the edge of her shorts, tracing the material with one nervous finger. "Actually, it was quite wonderful. I didn't know my body was capable of such feelings," she said slowly.

"What are you talking about? What about your other lovers? Did none of them ever satisfy you?"

She rubbed the edge of her shorts, wondering how to tell him. "Except for one fumbling foray into the realm of sex when I was in college, I, er, haven't had a very, um, active social life."

"Meaning?"

She threw him a look, a flush of embarrassed anger rising in her cheeks. "Meaning I've only done it once and it hurt."

He closed his eyes. He certainly had not been expecting that. This woman was the epitome of self-assurance and confidence. Hell, she'd lived in San Francisco all her life. Of course he'd expected her to have had lovers. Shoving his hat back from his face, he turned and looked at her.

"Dammit, you lived in San Francisco, a big, swinging city. You're pretty, successful . . ."

"What does that have to do with anything? You think I sleep around just because I'm from the city? Let me tell you something, cowboy, I have morals just the same as anyone else. And I don't—"

"Kelly, shut up. God, you have a mouth on you. Say one little thing and you jump in with both guns blazing."

"I wish I did have a gun. I'd take a shot at you."

"And I bet I know where."

"You'd better believe it, cowboy. Then you'd have a scar that would really gross people out."

He laughed. She was so mad she could hit him, and he laughed.

"Hell, I'd never show anyone," he said between breaths.

She smiled, then chuckled as his infectious laughter reached through her anger. It was an absurd picture.

Clamping her arm tightly against her side, she brought his fingers into contact with the soft swell of her breast. Slowly she stretched out her hand and rested it on his thigh.

"Kit, get some protection," she said softly, watching her fingers rub against the soft, faded denim.

"Have a care, darlin'. I can't use that leg, but it's not lost all its feeling."

She smiled, but couldn't quite meet his eyes. She felt like a brazen hussy, suggesting he get protection. Maybe she should get something, carry it with her, just in case.

"It might take a while," he said at last, the back of his fingers making the most of the contact with her softness. "Wouldn't have been a problem a few years ago. But now, dammit, I can't get anything from around here. After my display at the dance everyone would suspect you and I . . ."

She looked up and blushed. "Small town, huh?"

"You better believe it. It'd make the front page of the local paper. I told you I haven't had another woman since I was injured."

"So what if they know? We're grown up."

"I don't want gossip about you, Kelly," he said gently.

Her eyes stung with tears again, but for a different reason. No one had ever taken care of her before. She felt cherished.

"I said you were a pussycat." She smiled shyly.

"Now listen here." He dragged her across the seat, his hand suddenly hard on her arm, pulling her up against him, his hard thigh pressing against hers. "Men don't mind being called a tiger, or lion maybe, but I absolutely draw the line at pussycat." He glared at her.

She giggled. "You scare me."

His face softened and he released her arm to cup her chin in his hand, brushing his thumb over her lips.

"Go inside and stop being so sassy."

"Or?"

"Or your reputation can go hang. Molly Benson is about to fall out of her window watching us."

She giggled again and kissed against his thumb. "Thank you for taking me on my picnic. It was rather different from any I've gone on before. I didn't realize how differently you do things in the country."

"Get."

She slid across the seat and out the door. Taking her things from the back, she stood on the side of the driveway as he backed out, gazing after the truck long after it had disappeared from view.

Seeing the little black pony had helped. The next morning she began painting again, the sketches from yesterday just what she needed to bring the book to life. She concentrated on her work, and slowly the panels came to life.

Two days were uneventful, but productive. Kelly worked on the story line, blocked out pictures and began the soft watercolors that she used for illustrations. The book was taking shape and she would be finished before too many more weeks passed.

The strident ring of her phone shattered the peaceful afternoon. Dashing down the stairs, she wondered if it would be Kit, asking about her, seeing if she wanted to go out with him. She'd heard nothing from him since he'd dropped her off earlier in the week. Blast the man, he had to know she wanted to hear from him.

"Hi, Kelly. Sally Lockford."

Surprised at the wave of disappointment that swept through her, Kelly forced her thoughts away from Kit.

"We're having a small group for a barbecue next Friday. We'd like you to join us. Can you make it?"

She'd see him on Friday was her first gleeful thought when she finished talking to Sally. She had longed to ask after Kit, but was too shy, too unsure of their tenuous relationship to do that. It was enough she'd see him soon.

Sally had arranged for Beth and her husband to give Kelly a lift, and when they arrived at the Lockford ranch late Friday afternoon they were not the first. There were several cars parked on the grass, people already sitting on the deck, Kit in the center of the group.

Kelly recognized some of the other guests—Clint, Greg Martin, Bob and Mary Nash, whom she'd met at the dance. There were others, but she couldn't remember their names.

Sally came out the screen door with a tray of cold drinks in her hand just as Kelly and the Stapletons joined the group.

"Hi, glad you could make it. Kelly, do you know everyone?" She easily made the introductions, and Kelly tried desperately to remember all the names. If people wouldn't move around, she'd have a better chance.

"For you." Kelly handed Sally her latest story, about a little Chinese boy playing detective in San Francisco's Chinatown.

"Great. Julie'll love it."

"Not another book for Julie. I'm still hoarse from the last one," Kit protested, his eyes on Kelly, amusement and something else gleaming there. He'd had his eyes on her since she had arrived.

"Should I have brought you your own copy?" She smiled and walked toward him, unsure of her place here tonight.

Was the charade over? Or should she greet him as if they were lovers?

"Pull up a chair next to me, Kelly, darlin', and tell these folks about your writing," Kit said, glancing around the group. "Earlier this week we tracked down the Smiths' pony so she could get authenticity for her next story. Though all our picnic wasn't suitable for a child's book. Was it?" His smile was devilish, his look decidedly provocative.

Kelly saw Sally's look of surprise as Kit reached out to take her hand in his, threading his fingers through hers. She shook her head and smiled at the group, blood pounding through her at his touch. Had their picnic meant anything to him? Or was he just playacting here? How was she supposed to reply to his seductive innuendo?

"Dinner will be ready in about a half hour," Sally said to fill in the momentary silence. "We hired the Soames sisters to fix the side dishes and Pete is in charge of the barbecue." The tantalizing aroma of the meat cooking over the grill had been wafting around the house for some time. Kelly's stomach growled and she was glad they'd be eating soon. Maybe if she remembered she was only playing a part, she could manage to eat in peace. She had a hard time keeping her eyes off Kit. Laughing at his nonsense, preening before his blatant approval, and flirting. She must be doing something right—his look was definitely approving.

"Clint, would you get Kelly's present?" Kit asked, his eyes dancing as he studied her, interested in her reaction.

"What present?" Kelly turned in surprise.

"I bought you a peace offering," he said.

"What awful thing did you do, Kit?" Sally asked, looking between Kit and Kelly as if puzzled by their relationship.

"We had a small problem at the end of the picnic. I hope to make it up to her."

Kelly's face flamed. If he'd bought a box of . . .

Just then Beth said in strange voice, "Oh, Kelly."

She turned and looked, her heart catching in her throat as Clint led the small black pony around the side of the house. A bright blue ribbon was tied cockily on his mane.

Sam's ears were pricked as he looked around expectantly. Bewildered, Kelly looked back at Kit, his eyes on her as he watched for her reaction.

"Sam? For me?"

He nodded. "Got him yesterday. Had the devil's own time talking Will Smith out of him. But I convinced him their grandbaby wouldn't need a pony for years and I knew someone who needed one right now."

Kelly caught her bottom lip between her teeth as she rose and hurried gleefully across the veranda to the pony, hugging his neck, rubbing his forehead, laughing at the silly extravagance. Happiness flooded through her at the unexpected gesture. Had he known how much this would mean to her? She'd never had a pet in her life!

"Wouldn't a horse be more in order?" Beth asked, puzzled.

"No, this is perfect! Kit's good at doing wonderful things." Kelly threw him a saucy grin and ran back up the steps to him. Leaning down, she brushed her lips against his.

She'd meant it to be a light, thank-you kind of kiss, but he caught her head and held her against his mouth for a long, deep kiss, his fingers threading through her silky hair, holding her close. Taking his time, he made sure she and everyone there knew she'd been thoroughly kissed.

"What are you going to do with him, Kelly?" Sally asked as Kelly stood up in confusion.

"I don't know. I never had a pony before." Actually, she was having trouble moving her gaze from Kit's. Having trouble recognizing the other guests. His kiss was another of the wonderful things he did. She smiled at her new gift, her heart swelling at the unexpected pleasure she felt.

"I had a pony cart when I was a teenager," Beth said as she went down the stairs to inspect the pony. "I bet Dad still has it around. You could have it and Sam could pull you around. In fact, I bet Dad'll let you board him at our place."

"Sam stays here, no charge," Kit said. "How else can I make sure I see her often?"

Kelly was aware of the silence that dropped with his statement, then she smiled pertly and flirted with him. Her heart ached at the thought they were just pretending. But she never fooled herself. "Cowboy, I don't need the pony as an excuse to see you often."

Kit laughed, his eyes applauding her response.

Dinner was fun. Everyone had grown up around Taylorville except Kelly and Mike Stapleton, so they all knew each other and spent the meal recounting the most outrageous escapades of their youth. Kelly sat back and enjoyed the banter and backchat the others passed back and forth as they reminisced about childhood exploits, school activities and mutual friends. Their stories brought laughter and more memories from everyone. The stories Clint told about Kit were the most outlandish, though he swore they were all true.

Soon, however, Kelly began to feel left out. She didn't belong with this group. They had been friends forever. They all had families that lived in the area, could trace their roots back for generations, had shared memories and common interests. She had only a few vague memories of her mother, and then endless foster homes. She no longer belonged in San Francisco, but she didn't belong here, either.

Maybe she never would belong anywhere, she thought forlornly. They moved to sit on the deck later, after-dinner drinks and coffee in hand. The night air was soft and balmy, a slight breeze stirring. Kelly pushed her chair back a little from the loose circle, moving into the shadows. There wasn't much light, just the illumination spilling from the house and the faint light from a million scattered stars.

She could hear the gentle nicker of the horses in the corral. The stamping of a hoof. This was an alien setting for her. Was she foolish to think one day she'd fit in, belong?

She watched the others, listening avidly, but contributed nothing to the conversation, feeling out of place and lonely.

It was late when the first of the guests began to depart. Everyone had enjoyed the evening, but they were working people, with chores to see to in the morning, or a store to open, and they'd already stayed longer than they should have.

"I'll take Kelly home," Kit said easily when Beth and Mike rose to leave.

"It's on our way," Mike said. Beth nudged him.

"If it's okay with Kelly," she said.

"I'll go with Kit. Thanks for the ride here," Kelly said warmly, tantalizing sparks of anticipation dancing at the thought of being alone with Kit. Though she knew why Kit was doing this; she shouldn't let herself read anything more into it.

When the last of the other guests had departed, Kit turned to Kelly. "Want to see Sam again before you go?"

"Yes. I can't believe you got him for me! I've never had such a special gift. Did Clint put him in the corral?"

"Yes. Come on, I'll show you."

They walked down the ramp from the deck and around the house toward the corral at the back. The night was cooler now, the air still and scented with horses and dirt and dried hay. She heard the quiet clomp of horses in the corral, the gentle nicker from one a melodious sound in the quiet night. She walked toward the rail fencing. Overhead the stars were brilliant in the dark, clear sky. A serene feeling of peace, happiness and contentment pervaded the air.

Kit went toward the barn and flicked on a switch at the outside wall. Immediately the corral was flooded with bright light. Kelly stepped up on the fence and leaned against the top rail, watching her little pony. He ambled over toward her and she reached through the rails to rub his face.

"Looks small next to the horses, doesn't he?" Kit joined her.

"Yes. Will he be all right in there with them?" she asked. "They won't step on him, or anything, will they?"

"He'll be fine. Now you can join in when people talk of livestock and ranching. You'll have more in common with everyone around here," he said gently.

Kelly was touched he'd noticed she hadn't fit in tonight. And had wanted to make things easier for her. "I don't know much about taking care of him," she said as the pony ambled away.

"We'll show you. He won't take much care. Come on, I'll drive you home."

Kelly relaxed against the back of her seat when she was in the truck, pleasantly tired after a long day. It was dark as Kit pulled away from the house. The headlights slashed the inky night ahead of them, the surrounding hills shadowy and shapeless. After a couple of turns, Kit slowed, drawing to a stop. He clicked off the lights, plunging them into darkness.

"Why have we stopped?" Kelly asked. Her eyes strained to see something besides the stars in the sky.

"I wanted to explain to you about Althea and our charade."

"I thought you had. This whole charade is for her benefit."

"Because of her, yes, but not just for her. It's for others, too."

Kelly still couldn't see him clearly, just a silhouette against the starlight.

"Sally is an incurable romantic. She sees Althea and me as star-crossed lovers, torn apart by a huge misunderstanding. She's hoping for rekindled happiness." Kit's voice was hard, sardonic.

"And you don't?" Kelly said.

"For the last couple of years I've been rebuilding my life. It's different from what I'd always expected. It's taking a long time. I'm doing okay. But I haven't dealt with the personal side, the romantic side as Sally puts it. Before I met you I didn't think I could."

"Did the injuries . . ."

He shook his head. Kelly could just see it in the faint light. Her eyes were growing more adjusted to the feeble light.

"I was gored pretty badly, but the son of a bitch missed that part. Hell, I don't want to talk about sex. I'm trying to tell you why I want to keep Althea at bay. Why we need to continue the charade, why it's so important to me." Would she buy it? It had started out that way, as a charade to assuage his pride. Now he knew he was just using it as an excuse to spend time with Kelly. Without her agreement to help, he really didn't know if she'd see him as much, and he craved her companionship. He'd never admit it, of course. Not to anyone. But for as long as she was willing, he'd keep up the pretense.

"Because Althea was so awful when you got hurt?" Kelly clarified.

"That and I don't want her pity or condescension. I know how her mind works. She's a beautiful woman, and knows it. And uses that to get what she wants. I think she and most of the other people in town believe I'm still carrying the torch for her."

"And are you?" Kelly held her breath, her heartbeat heavy against her chest.

"No, dammit, haven't you been listening to anything I've said?" He lifted his hat from his head and ran his fingers through his hair in frustration, slamming the hat back on hard. "God, you're as bad as Sally." But at least she didn't suspect the real reason for his pretense.

"No, I'm not. I just want to understand where we stand with this make-believe romance you want. I thought I was to pretend to be your girlfriend. Half the time I don't know if I'm supposed to be in love with you or just a casual friend. If you truly don't want her, then I'll do all I can to show everybody you are over her. But if you think the two of you can get back together, let's stop this charade now, before it goes any further."

Before I have a chance to fall in love with you and get hurt.

Seven

"I want Althea to be convinced once and for all that it's all over between us. I don't want her hanging around me, acting solicitous, patronizing me. Dammit, I won't have her calling Sally every day to check up on me. I need Sally to believe we are involved so she can make it very clear to Allie. It isn't something we just turn on and off whenever Althea is around. We need to play it for all it's worth around everyone."

"Okay, so we pretend for a while longer, and around everybody. How long is Althea going to be here?"

"I don't know. She said something about it depending on things. Maybe if she sees I'm not interested, she'll leave that much sooner."

"Maybe." Kelly thought it might take a lot to convince Althea, if she had really set her sights on Kit.

"I appreciate your help, Kelly. I won't repay you by taking advantage of you again." His voice was low and the words sounded rehearsed.

Kelly's amused face tried to see him, but it was just too dark. She thought he was staring straight ahead and she knew him well enough to imagine his expression.

"You mean no sex? No more kisses, caresses . . ."

"That's exactly what I mean." He only hoped he could do it. Even now when he was promising to stay away from her his hand itched to hold her, his mouth wanted to plunder her softness, taste her sweetness, feel the silky texture of her skin, learn all the hot secrets she alone held. He tightened his fists on the wheel.

"You're sure stupid sometimes, Kit," she said, amusement lacing her voice.

His head snapped around as he tried to see her in the darkness. His eyes narrowed, but he couldn't make her out in the stygian night.

"I have it on excellent authority that no woman would want me. That from a woman who once professed to love me."

"Nonsense. If she loved you nothing on earth would have kept her away from you, no matter what happened. If you'd lost both legs and both arms and she loved you she would have been there for you. And you're a damn fool if you believe otherwise. Maybe that bull addled your brains, as well. Did the doctors check that?"

"*Jesus*. Are there any more insults you want to hurl at me? I've never met anyone as insulting as you in my entire life! The first words out of your mouth were an insult and you haven't slowed down since."

She laughed softly, reaching out to trail her fingers lightly down his arm, feeling the leashed energy, the tightly coiled muscles.

"Just because you're stubborn and hardheaded and act like an idiot and a fool sometimes, are people supposed to tiptoe around that and keep quiet?" she asked teasingly.

He sighed and leaned back in the seat, quiet for a long time. "Everyone else has since the accident." His reply was low, bitter.

"They're coddling you, Kit. And you don't need it. I think it's become a habit now," she replied seriously.

"God help the man who tries to court you. You've a hard tongue in you."

She laughed again, squeezing his arm gently. "I hope he comes along soon. I'm not getting any younger."

"He'd need to be strong to take you on."

"Yes, strong and handsome and full of life. Appreciating me and what I do as I'll appreciate him and what he does."

He started the truck and flicked on the headlights. She could see him now, in the illumination from the dashboard. His expression was closed, impassive, his jaw hard.

"What else?" He pulled away from the side of the road and headed toward town.

"I don't know. I don't have an ideal man in mind, just some characteristics." She didn't mention her desire for a large family, and most of all a feeling of belonging.

"He'd need to walk," Kit said bitterly.

She paused, struck again by his stupidity. Were all men so blind? Her heart pounding, she said gently, "Actually, it isn't one of the requirements. I don't care if he walks, hears, or sees, as long as he loves me to distraction and I love him."

He didn't respond. The ride was silent. Kelly thought of all the things he'd said. Why had he explained it to her? Was he looking for something more? Yet with the same breath he was talking about staying away from her. She didn't understand what he wanted. Part of her was afraid to ask him. Kit claimed he only wanted her to pretend they were involved, but when he took her in his arms it didn't feel like pretend. Surely he felt something for her, didn't he? Maybe if they kept up the game long enough even this hardheaded cowboy would admit he wanted her.

Before too long they could see lights in the distance. They were almost at Kelly's place.

"You're driving very sedately, for you," she said, hoping to tease him into a better mood. She hadn't meant to insult him into a bad temper, just shake him up a bit.

"You're enough danger. I don't need to risk my neck with you in the truck by driving fast."

"Is that why you drive fast, to risk your neck?"

"No." He was quiet for a few seconds, then shook his head. "It's hard to explain. I was used to doing things, exciting things, riding in the rodeo, living in the fast lane, living on the edge. Now I have nothing. I can't do any of that. I'm confined to a snail's pace. Driving is the only thing where I still have some control. The only thing where I can capture some of the essence of what I had before, speed. It's as close as I get to excitement anymore."

"Don't you ride horses?"

"Now you're the one who's stupid. What do you think?"

She stared at him a moment, then nodded. "You're right, I'm sorry I insulted you. It's not a nice feeling when someone calls you stupid. Especially when I know I'm not. Though I still think you are sometimes." She couldn't resist. "But I don't understand about riding. I thought stock horses were superbly trained. I've seen pictures and documentaries of handicapped kids riding. Why don't you? You even have some use of your legs."

"Not enough to ride."

"Tie yourself into the saddle."

"Sure, and if the horse stumbles and rolls, get crushed?"

"There's that element of danger you're looking for. Have you ever tried?"

"No. Next time I'll let Beth and Mike bring you home." He turned in to her driveway.

"Thank you again for Sam. I'll come out to the ranch on Sunday to see him, if I can."

"Yeah. Did you understand what I was leading up to when talking about Althea?"

"You want her to know you are no longer interested."

"Right. But we can't pretend just when she's around."

"Yet you also said no kisses."

He was silent for a moment. "We need to show a certain amount of affection in public. Purely for show."

"So if Molly Benson is watching from her window now, we should act as if we were interested in each other so she can spread gossip and Althea will hear about it, right?" Kelly asked softly, sliding closer to him on the seat.

"Don't push me, Kelly."

"Now how can we convince anyone you're taken if we don't exchange at least a few chaste kisses?"

"Honey, your kisses are anything but chaste." He slid his hand beneath the heavy hair on her neck and rubbed her skin gently, slowly pulling her closer, unable to resist the pull of attraction that flared any time she was near him.

Little nibbles at the corner of her mouth raised desires she hadn't known before, causing her mouth to ache with physical longing for his. She turned, trying to capture his lips with hers, but he evaded them, placing feather-light kisses on her cheeks, nibbling again at her jaw, her earlobe.

"God, Kit, you're driving me crazy." Her voice was low, urgent, her hands clutching at him.

"I could eat you up!"

She clasped her hands on either side of his head and held him still, fastening her mouth against his in desperate need.

He assuaged the aching need of her mouth but built a stronger hunger elsewhere. His lips moved against hers, parting them to permit his tongue access to the sweet recesses of her hot mouth. He opened his wide, demanding the same from her, giving her long, drugging kisses, intensifying her emotions, building her hunger.

She ached for closeness, but the confines of the truck and the steering wheel made it impossible. Her hands ran over his cheeks, slightly rough now with a day's growth of beard. They kneaded his shoulders, his muscular arms, sought the buttons of his shirt.

He pulled back and kissed her lightly on her warm lips, gathering her hands in his, stopping their seeking. Another minute of this and he'd lose all control.

"No more, honey. That will have to satisfy Molly."

Kelly felt as if he'd slapped her. Had he only done it to fool Molly? Had it only been for show, to reinforce the charade for Althea? She felt sick. Wrenching open the door, she stumbled from the truck, slamming the door behind her. Walking swiftly around the front, passing in the glaring headlights, she averted her face from his view.

She stormed up her walkway and into her house, head held high. Slamming her own door in frustration, she almost screamed. But it was her own fault. She'd agreed to the pretense. She'd even brought up Molly at the window, when that woman must have been in bed asleep hours ago. She'd wanted his kisses, but she'd wanted them to mean something. Not just a means to get back to Althea to prove he was over her.

She was wrong. Kit wasn't a fool—she was. And the next time she saw him she'd let him know their deal was off. He'd have to find another way to get back at Althea. Kelly wasn't playing anymore. She didn't want to be kissed because of some other woman. She wanted him to kiss her for herself!

Sunday morning Kelly attended the local church. Since she was trying to fit into the community she reasoned the sooner she was involved in various aspects, the sooner people would accept her. She was pleased to recognize people she'd met the past few weeks, and their greetings made her feel welcomed.

She spoke with Clint and Sally after church. There was no sign of Kit, and Kelly refused to ask after him.

"You coming out to our place this afternoon?" Sally asked as they got ready to leave. "I know you want to see Sam."

"Yes, if I won't be in the way," Kelly said, enjoying the groups of people talking on the lawn in front of the old church. Her eyes darted around, taking in everything, thinking how like a Norman Rockwell setting it was. Yet it was real.

"No problem. I'll show you how to do everything you need with a pony. Come around two."

"See you then."

When Kelly arrived at the ranch, Kit's truck was missing. She didn't see Clint, either, but Sally enthusiastically greeted her and led the way to the barn.

Time sped by. Kelly learned how to groom the pony and pick his hooves. Sally explained about shots and vet visits, feedings and shoeing.

"Not that you have to worry about all that. I'm sure Kit will take care of everything, but it's good to know."

Kelly nodded, wondering who would take care of Sam when she and Kit no longer played their charade. She paused a moment, her hand on the silky pony. She was going to end that next time she saw him. Maybe she should see if Beth's father could board the pony right away.

"I have to go," Kelly said when Sally suggested they share iced tea on the deck.

"Come any time. If no one's home, just come back to the barn. We don't keep anything locked. You can use any of the equipment."

And so for the next couple of days, Kelly spent her mornings working on the book and her afternoons at the Lockford ranch working with her pony. Kit was conspicuously absent at each visit, though Kelly stalled as late as she could each day without being obvious about it.

Wednesday she worked at home all day, finishing her book just before dinner. It had gone faster than any book she'd completed before and she was pleased with the result. Excited, she called her agent.

Judith was thrilled to hear the book was already finished. "That's the quickest I've known you to do one. Maybe being in the country will be great for your work."

"Reserve judgment until you see it. It may not be something you think you can sell. I thought I'd come in to the city tomorrow, bring you the manuscript and do some shopping."

"Great. Plan to stay the night."

"Sure. Let's go to a sushi bar for dinner. I'm longing for some food I can't get here."

"You're in beef country there. We'll eat every meal at a different place."

"You're on!" Kelly smiled, looking forward to visiting with Judith, looking forward to seeing San Francisco. It had been over a month since she had moved from the city. It didn't seem possible.

Early the next morning, dressed up in what she now thought of as her city clothes, Kelly headed west. It felt great to dress up again. Though she was comfortable in the shorts and jeans she now wore, she liked dressing up.

The drive was pleasant through the central valley and over the Altamont Pass into the Bay Area. As she drew closer and closer to the city, Kelly was constantly reminded how different the sleepy area in Tuolumne County was. There the rolling hills were covered with grass and trees and cattle. Here every hillside was covered with homes. Traffic was heavy, even though rush hour had long passed. She could feel the energy of the city as she drew nearer. Almost before she realized it she was parking in the Stockton Street garage and on her way to meet Judith.

Kelly had worn a warm suit. The hot central valley weather was not found along the coast in summer. Here the wind was cold, the tall buildings hid the sun and the ocean fog kept the temperatures cool.

Judith enthused over the paintings, the story line. Scanning it quickly at first, then slowly, critically studying each setting, she smiled smugly. "Probably the best you've done so far," she told Kelly as she turned the pages.

Kelly smiled. Suddenly she wanted to share Judith's assessment with Kit. The smile faded. Would he even care? She was thinking about him too much. Wasn't she planning to tell him the charade was over?

The day whirled by. Judith took Kelly to lunch at a favorite sushi bar and caught her up on all the news of mutual friends. When Judith went back to work, Kelly visited her old neighborhood until time to meet Judith for dinner.

They ate in Chinatown and Kelly relished the chow fun, sweet and sour pork and spicy Mongolian beef. She relished the diversity of the food in San Francisco, and hadn't realized how much she missed the opportunity for variety until she no longer had it.

Otherwise, she found she'd missed little about the city. It was beautiful, clear and cool, giving its best face for the tourists who flocked to see it. But the street people downtown reduced a lot of the charm. Traffic was worse than she remembered. The indifference from everyone was almost shocking after the friendliness in Taylorville.

She enjoyed her two days, but was not unhappy to leave. She hadn't fully realized it before, but Taylorville had become home.

Kelly was surprised to see Kit's truck parked in her driveway as she approached her house late Friday afternoon. Slowly she pulled in behind him. The truck was empty. She looked at her porch. Not there.

As she slid from the car, she wondered where he was. Was he waiting for her? How had he known she was coming home at this time? She still wore a blue silk dress. It was a little warm for the heat in Taylorville, and she had planned to change as soon as she reached home. But first she'd look for him.

As she walked up the driveway she heard voices in the back. Curious, she walked along the side of her house and paused. Kit was sitting beneath the large oak with Molly. Both were drinking iced tea and seemed content to relax in the shade.

Kit saw her as soon as she appeared, and sat up.

"Where the hell have you been?" he asked, glaring at her.

Kelly smiled and walked slowly across the grass, her high heels sinking into the dirt with each step. She knew she looked good. Her hair was French braided to keep it from her face, her makeup was impeccable. It was her usual style for the city. Would he see any difference in her?

"Hello, Molly, Kit. Nice to see you both," Kelly said deliberately, ignoring his outburst.

Kit scowled, remembering her comment a while ago about not greeting people.

"Is this one of those occasions when you haven't seen someone for a while?" he asked.

"Yes, it is." She smiled at him, holding his gaze, wondering if he'd give in.

"Hello, Kelly Adams. It is nice to see you after so long a time. Where the hell have you been for two days?"

He had started out in a falsetto, but ended up in a deep growl and she knew better than to push her luck any further.

Conscious of Molly's curious eyes, Kelly crossed the rest of the way and leaned over to kiss Kit. "I went to San Francisco. I think I've sold my pony book."

"You might have let someone know," he said darkly, looking at the tea.

Kelly dragged another chair into the group and sat down, glancing from him to Molly. "I rather think you are right about that, Kit. But I'm not used to accounting for myself to others."

"That's wonderful about your book, Kelly," Molly broke in, trying to calm the storm that seemed to be brewing. She looked at Kit to concur, but he remained silent. Finally she gave a small sigh.

"I'll be going. I guess you two want to be alone."

Kelly smiled and said goodbye, watching as the older woman walked back to her own house.

"Do we want to be alone?" she asked once the back door had closed behind Molly Benson.

"Come closer, Miss Sassy-mouth, and see what I want," he said, placing his glass on the grass beside his chair.

Kelly studied him for a moment, trying to gauge his mood. Feeling on top of the world because of her visit to San Francisco, she slowly stood and walked over, daring to sit in his lap.

Kit was surprised, but only for a second. His arms came around her and he pulled her down against his chest, her head nestling against his shoulder and neck.

"I've been alone and on my own for so long I didn't even think to let anyone know I was going into the city for a couple of days."

"We all worried about you. Sally didn't know why you hadn't been out to see the pony. Molly didn't know where you'd gone. I asked everyone that knew you."

"You weren't worried about me, too, were you?" she asked lightly, breathing in the scent of him, warm and masculine. Her heart rate increased.

"No." One hand slowly slid up and down her arm while his other hand held her hip firmly. "This dress feels as soft as your skin," he said quietly.

"It's silk," she said closing her eyes. Was this heaven? Had she taken a wrong turn somewhere and ended up in heaven?

"It feels like you do all over." His voice was low and Kelly felt a surge of desire sweep through her. She remembered every touch of his hands and fingers and mouth that day of the picnic. Her body heated in response and she shifted uneasily, not wanting him to know.

"Is this for Molly Benson's benefit?" she asked.

"I rather think it's for mine."

She looked up at him at that and smiled, her finger gently tracing the outline of his mouth.

"I couldn't wait to tell you the news about my book," she said shyly.

"I'm proud of you, honey. You're so talented. I wish I was."

"I think you are, only in other areas." She pulled his lip a little and slipped her finger into his mouth. His tongue greeted her and his lips closed over the finger.

Kelly tilted her head, pulling her hand away, only to reach behind him and urge him toward her.

He needed no coaxing. His mouth covered hers in a rough kiss, full of desire and passion. She reveled in his touch, conscious his hands were still, holding her close to him, feeling the strength of his chest against hers, the power of his shoulders and the growing hardness in his lap.

Pulling back, breathing hard, she gazed up into his glittering eyes.

"Was that enough for Molly, do you think?" Kit asked lazily as he brought the brim of his hat down to shade his eyes.

Kelly struggled to get up. But he held her hard against him. She hit him with her fist and he chuckled. "Damn you. Let me up. That's plenty for Molly," she said through gritted teeth. He made her so mad.

"Good, then the rest is for us." He swept his hat from his head and gathered her closer, his mouth plundering her halfhearted resistance and sweeping her along with an intensity that threatened to flame out of control. It was hot and exciting and demanding. She moved against him, responding, rising to the passion he built between them. Kelly wanted to float on the cloud of delight and bliss that his touch brought. All thoughts of ending the charade fled. Not yet. She wouldn't stop just yet.

But his kiss eased, ended. He cradled her head against his shoulder.

"You look pretty. Is that how you dress in the big city?"

"Yes." Her breathing was ragged, her heart pounded, heat washed through her. She wanted him, she ached for him. Closing her eyes she tried to imprint every inch of her skin with the feel of Kit. His breathing fanned her cheeks, her heart pounded beneath her breast, his hands burned through her skin. Would he come inside with her?

"Do you miss the city?" he asked, his voice sounding almost hollow.

"No." How could he carry on a conversation? She wanted to scream. Taking a deep breath, she tried to act normal. "In fact, I felt quite the country bumpkin when I was there. We ate at a different restaurant for each meal and I enjoyed that. But the traffic was awful. The street people are panhandling worse than ever and no one was friendly. I was glad to visit, but happy to come home."

"Umm, good. I got the cart from Beth's dad. Come out to the ranch and see if Sam can use it."

"I can't today. I'm too tired. It was a long drive and the traffic was worse than usual because it's Friday. Can I come in the morning?"

"Sure, though Clint and Sally are driving down to Sonora in the morning for some serious shopping."

"I'll come in the early afternoon, then." Slowly she pushed herself up and stood, trying to straighten her hopelessly wrinkled dress. Reluctant to bid him farewell, she was already anticipating tomorrow.

The yard surrounding the Lockford house was deserted the next afternoon when Kelly arrived. Kit's truck was parked to one side, and the one that Clint used was gone. The day was sunny and hot, with a slight breeze from the west to make it tolerable. She sat in her car for a long moment, expecting Kit to come to greet her.

But there was no movement, only the silence of the hot afternoon.

Climbing out, Kelly headed for the front door. It was open. Kelly peered through the screen, but the house was empty. Kelly rapped on wood and waited.

Looking around, she wondered if Kit was in the barn. She walked around the house and called him. No answer. The entire place seemed deserted. Had he gone with Clint and Sally?

She went back to the front door and rapped again.

She could hear music quietly playing down the hall. Opening the screen door, she stepped inside. Walking toward the music she came to Kit's room.

He was lying on a big bed, clothed in shirt and jeans, an open *Stockman's Journal* lying across his chest. He was asleep.

Kelly glanced curiously around his room. There was a trapezelike contraption over his bed, a wheelchair nearby, and the crutches leaned against the headboard. His room was decorated in dark blues and browns, masculine and cozy. There was an elaborate stereo system along one wall, and a big TV with VCR positioned to be watched from bed.

Her heart ached. How many hours had he lain in bed, not able to be outdoors, as he liked? Not living on the edge as he had done before, but confined to a room?

She walked over to the bed. It was higher than a normal bed, long and wide. She leaned over and brushed her lips against his.

His eyes opened.

She glanced down the length of him, looked back up to meet his eyes. "So this is how cowboys work, huh?" she said, smiling down at his look.

He let his eyes roam over her in the insolent manner that infuriated her so much. His eyes darkened as he took in the fullness of her breasts, the way the white top clung lovingly to her figure, tapering to her slim waist before flaring to her softly rounded hips.

"Know me again," she said, reaching out to cup his chin and raise his face to hers, tingling all over from his look.

His grin was pure wickedness. "Don't you knock?"

"I did. Don't you stay awake when you expect company?"

"I was reading up on range management." He indicated the magazine.

"I could tell. If now isn't convenient for me I can come back another time."

"Now's fine." Kit ran the fingers of one hand through his hair in exasperation. He hadn't meant to fall asleep. He'd just been killing time until her arrival.

"Are you sure you'd rather work with the pony than read up on range management? What do you want to do?" she asked, her eyes twinkling.

Eight

"What do you want, Kelly?"

"You," she whispered, feeling brazen and daring.

He flung the magazine away and reached for her, drawing her across his chest to lie beside him on the rich brown coverlet. Propping himself up on one arm, he looked down at her, his right arm pinioning her to the bed. Kelly made no protest, only smiled at him. She wasn't afraid. Her arms came up to reach around his neck and pull him down on top of her.

She saw his eyes spark with a deep flame before his head blocked the light as his warm mouth covered hers. His touch was light as he placed small kisses against her mouth, her cheeks, her throat.

Kelly delighted in his gentle touch, savoring the anticipation that built. He wouldn't be gentle for long, she knew. Desire flooded through her, excitement and expectation swamped every inch of her. She tightened her grip, toppling him over to lie heavily against her as his mouth roughly covered hers, seeking the smoldering heat he knew waited beneath her surface.

His hard tongue evoked an involuntary response from her, as he ravaged all resistance. Her senses reeled as she was taken by surprise at the intensity of feelings that overwhelmed her. His heat swept through the light cotton top and the jeans she was wearing, searing her flesh as he had that day on the hilltop. Her mouth moved beneath his as she sought to build the same fiery intensity in him as he built in her.

When his hand brushed down from her hair to her side and tugged the shirt from her jeans, her heart lurched. Her own hands were frantic to open his shirt. She wanted his chest against hers, wanted to feel that wiry hair against the sensitized tips of her breasts. Wanted to feel his hard muscles against her yielding softness.

Ah, his hand was on her bare midriff. Her nerve endings tingled with his touch, longed for more. She pulled back a little to give him access to her breasts, her hand pulling his up her body.

"You're wearing a bra," he said as he leaned back and rolled her onto her side to unfasten it.

"I do sometimes," she said testily. Damn, why had she today?

With the release, she sighed and rolled onto her back, pushing his buttons through the last holes and spreading the shirt from his shoulders. Kit sat up and whipped off his shirt, flinging it across the room.

He pulled her up and stripped off her shirt and bra together, pulling her against him, her softness covered by his strength as he gently lay back down on top of her.

"If you don't want to get into more trouble than you can handle, we'd better stop now," he said as his mouth moved over one throbbing mound, his tongue licking the satiny texture of her skin, tasting the essence of her. He moved up the slope to the thrusting tip and hesitated, his eyes looking up into hers.

"I don't want to stop," she whispered, threading her fingers into his thick hair and urging his face down to her. She moaned softly as his mouth captured the aching nub and gently began to torment it. Sensations flooded through her as his touch excited, intoxicated. His mouth was seething with banked fires, passion she'd known only once before—in his arms.

He eased up and moved to the other breast while her hands moved lovingly over his strong shoulders, feeling the muscles tense and relax beneath her touch. When his hand moved across her abdomen and down to the edge of her jeans, Kelly moved her hips, twisting and raising up, wanting his touch all over her. His hard hands trailed fire in their wake and she wanted more. Heat rose from deep within her, and she was losing cognitive thought as her body began to float on an unexplored sea of sensuous delights, buoyed by emotions and tactile sensations never known before. Tantalized by the promise of wonders to come, she moved against him, dying for him to love her.

When he slipped down the zipper of her jeans and peeled the tight denims off her hips, a jolt like an electric pulse caused her to arch against him. She was drowning in the deep pleasure of her own body, the pleasure he alone brought.

She arched against him again, her hands learning his back, coming around the strong side of his ribs to rake her fingers against the crisp hair that covered his chest. Finding his own dark nipples, she caressed them, moving beneath him on the bed, wanting more, more.

His hand cupped her bottom, lifting her slightly, sliding over the smooth taut skin. Coming around to the front, he traced the junction of her thighs with her hips, slipping between them, fingers tangling in the soft curls that guarded her femininity.

Kelly's mouth opened wide for his kiss, tasting him again, drinking in the pleasure he offered. She functioned only at a sensual level now, his body in control, reveling in the touch of his skin, the hot male scent filling her nostrils, the taste of his mouth in hers.

Her hands roamed lower over his chest, down the hard muscles of his belly, finding and fumbling with the catch of his jeans. He paused and Kelly held her breath. She'd die if he stopped now. Dimly she remembered his warning at the picnic, that his scars were bad. But she didn't care. She wanted him—she couldn't stop now.

Ignoring his hesitation, her hands continued. Sighing in relief when the zipper was down, she pushed against the top of the jeans.

Kit hesitated only a moment, then he assisted and was soon as naked as she. Kelly opened her eyes to gaze into his. She was surprised at the passionate glaze in his look, the depth of the blue in his eyes drawing her in, bathing her with awareness, heightening the electric pulse that seemed to throb deep in her soul. She smiled seductively, slowly letting her eyelids drift down as her hand drifted lower on his body. Encountering the rough, scarred skin, she skimmed over it, seeking the heart of his being at the moment and gently encircling him.

She was hot and damp and ready. She moved against him to let him know how much she wanted him.

"Hold on." He reached across to his nightstand and withdrew a foil packet from the drawer. In only a second he was ready.

"Now, darlin'," he said, and moved over her.

The seething flame of his passion transferred to her as she was caught up in the storm of his lovemaking. His hands evoked rippling waves of erotic excitement through her nerve endings, his tongue mated with hers and her body met his thrusts, rising and falling in the rhythm as old as mankind.

He captured her hands and held them on either side of her face as he plunged into her, withdrew slightly and plunged again. She was alive, tingling with pure sensation. She had never felt like this before, never known there could be such heights. Knowing she would melt into a fiery mass of shivering ecstasy, Kelly reveled in the enchantment. She gloried in the feel of him deep within her, the spiraling sensations taking her higher and higher until she exploded into fragments of pure gossamer and light. Shuddering again and again, she moaned her release, never wanting the moment to end.

He drew his head back, arching against her as he reached his own climax, and Kelly gloried in his pleasure, deeply moved she could bring satisfaction to so virile a man.

He collapsed on top of her, both breathing hard. Releasing her hands, he slipped his hands beneath her back, arching her a bit so her breasts were raised, and sank his head against her neck. Kelly encircled his damp skin, her fingers idly rubbing against the strong muscles of his back, her eyes closed, imprinting each separate sensation in her mind—the feel of his strong arms holding her, the hot breath puffing against her neck, the weight of him pressing her into the bed, the warmth where they were joined. She never wanted to forget. She knew she never would.

"Incredible!" Kit said softly against her skin, his lips nibbling the column of her neck. He raised up on his elbows, tilting Kelly tighter against him, and looked down at her.

She was exhausted, wanting only to savor the magic they'd just made. She looked up at him, knowing the love that consumed her must be reflected in her eyes, but unable to hide it. She smiled and nodded slightly, slowly, her lids drifting closed.

Kelly slept.

Damn! He never should have gone so far. Not that it hadn't been wonderful. Incredible, just as he'd said. But now he was in a fix. Slowly Kit withdrew and rolled over on his side, his eyes still on the sleeping woman beside him. She was incredibly lovely, flushed rosy from love, sleeping so trustfully beside him. He reached across her and drew the side of the coverlet over her to keep her warm. Punching up his pillow, he scooted against it and crossed his arms over his chest. What would she do when she awoke, though? When she saw the extent of his scars, when the irrationality of passion had waned and cold hard reality faced them.

His stomach tightened. He knew. She'd try to pretend it didn't matter, but he knew better. He looked with frustration at his jeans and shirt, scattered across his room with the force of his throw. Damn, he couldn't get them and put them on by himself without waking her.

And he hated the thought she'd see him.

Yet there was nothing he could do except steel himself against the pain, try to pretend it didn't matter. That he only wanted one time with her. That he wouldn't give all he owned to be a whole man who could love her to the end of time.

She murmured in her sleep, turning to her side seeking him.

He had to be ready when she awoke, but he had until then to pretend things were normal. And he was only human, he thought as he gazed at her with a deep hunger in his eyes. Gathering her close, he lay down, resting her head against his shoulder, draping one of her arms across his chest. He flicked the covers so they sheltered them both. And closed his eyes, relishing the feeling of this soft, sexy woman in his arms.

When Kelly stirred, Kit was awake. He tightened his arm a second before relaxing and moving away. The time was here and he still wasn't ready.

Her hand moved against his chest, moved lower and dipped into his navel. "Are you going to show me how to hook Sam up to the cart?" she asked softly, loving the feel of him against her skin, the steady rise and fall as he breathed, the heat that still burned her.

"Hitch. Yeah, that's why you came, isn't it?"

She kissed his chest and tilted back her head to see him. "Maybe."

He cocked an eyebrow. "Why else?"

"Is this an act, or are you naturally this dumb?" she asked, teasing him.

"Now why would I think that after an afternoon of making love you'd be all sweetness and light and forget the insults for a while?"

She laughed. "I should be fawning all over you, shouldn't I? Telling you how wonderful you are and how grand the afternoon's been and how I can't wait until next time...."

"Shut up."

She sat up, pushing her hair out of her face and looking at him, her head inclined consideringly. Seeing the vulnerability behind his eyes, her heart ached.

She touched his arm lightly. "It was the most wonderful experience I've ever had in my life," she said sincerely.

"Yeah, well, I gave it my best shot."

"It was the best. Are we going to see Sam now?" she asked.

"Sure. Get dressed, then I'll come out when I'm dressed."

"Oh, no, buster. If we are intimate enough to undress each other, we are intimate enough to dress each other!" she said firmly, bouncing off the bed and walking around the room picking up their clothing.

Kit said nothing, keeping the coverlet firmly across his waist as he watched her. She moved unselfconsciously as she leaned over or stooped to gather shirts, jeans, underwear. She put them all on the bed and drew her own panties on first. She caught his eyes watching her and smiled, holding his gaze as she slowly drew on one sock, then another, her breasts free and pert under his gaze. Then she drew on her jeans, sliding them over her hips, and leaving the zipper undone.

Kit swallowed. It was as exciting as a striptease. She was sexy as hell and must know what she was doing to him. Leaving her bra on the bed, she slipped the shirt on over her head. Pulling it down, she smoothed over her breasts, the nipples pushing against the soft cotton as if asking for release.

"Your turn," she said, handing him his jeans and briefs.

"Kelly..." he said with a hint of desperation in his voice.

She moved near the head of the bed and pulled down the right side of her jeans and panties. "Here's my scar," she said, pointing to a thin line approximately four inches long. "Where are yours?"

Kit took a deep breath and tossed back the covers, exposing the crisscross of scars along his hip, thigh and stomach.

"If that isn't just like some damn macho cowboy, always wanting to top everybody," she said in disgust when she saw the puckered skin and scar tissue.

Then she leaned over and dropped a kiss on the worst of them. Kit was shocked. Even more so when she looked up at him and said, "I'm sorry you were hurt, but if it kept you from Althea and saved you for me, it wasn't all bad." Then she pulled up her jeans and zipped them closed.

"Hurry up, I want to see Sam."

"These are awful," he said, stunned at her lack of revulsion.

"If you say so. I want to go see the pony. If you want me to get sick or have a hissy fit, it'll have to be later." She put on her shoes and sat in his wheelchair while he dressed, fascinated to see how he managed.

He was puzzled. Could it be the scars really didn't repulse her? That they weren't as bad as Althea had made him think? But as he turned to get out of bed, he knew it didn't matter. He still wasn't a whole man. Reaching for the crutches, he felt his mood turn black. He didn't need her presence around him to show him what he was missing. What he would always miss.

Kelly walked out to the barn, her spirits high. She loved him! She doubted she'd even notice the scars in the future. They weren't as awful as he'd led her to believe, and they really didn't matter. They were a part of Kit and she accepted him as he was. Loved him as he was. She hesitated when that thought crashed through her. It was a mistake. He'd never given any indication he wanted anything more from her than protection from Althea. Temporary protection, at that.

She walked on. It didn't matter. One couldn't dictate who to love and who not to. She'd love him the best she could and if nothing came of it, she'd still have memories to cherish.

Could she make him love her? Make him want her so badly he'd do anything she wanted? Like consider marriage?

Whew, slow down, she thought. That would scare him into the next county. Her thoughts churning, she had a hard time giving her full attention to the lesson.

Kit patiently showed Kelly how to hitch the pony to the cart, and how to unhitch him. They practiced over and over until Kelly could manage it on her own without any prompting. If he was exasperated by her slowness, he gave no sign. He was patient and encouraging as he taught her what she needed to know.

"Now take him by the halter and lead him around a bit, get him used to pulling it," Kit said when he was satisfied she could hitch Sam correctly.

He leaned back against the corral fence and watched as she led Sam out of the barn and around the yard. Sam followed docilely at first, but then he grew fitful, kicking out his hind legs, trying to dislodge his unusual burden.

"Whoa, honey, it's okay." Kelly stopped, patted him and talked softly to him until he calmed down. Then she started again. A few more steps and Sam reared, prancing, trying to dislodge the cart.

"Hold on to him, Kelly, don't let him pull away. He'll get used to it," Kit called.

So the pattern repeated. They'd walk a few steps, then Sam would try to escape. Kelly quieted him, started again.

"That's enough for today," Kit called after two complete turns around the yard without any problem. He came over. "I'll hold him while you unhitch him. Good boy, Sam, you'll be pulling this in no time." Kit's large hands gently rubbed the pony's face, and his voice was soft.

"Will he really pull it?" she asked, discouraged.

"Sure, if you keep working with him until he no longer gives you any trouble. Then you can try riding in the cart. He'll get used to it in no time."

Kelly maneuvered the cart to the side of the barn, out of the way of the ranch work, while Kit led Sam to the corral. He opened the gate and let the pony in, leaning on the closed gate and watching the horses. Kelly joined him, peering through the bars, her glance going once or twice to Kit.

"You should try riding."

"I told you I can't." His voice was hard.

"The doctors said you wouldn't walk, if I heard what you said. You proved them wrong. Why not prove yourself wrong and ride a horse? Not some wild stallion that you might have ridden in a rodeo, but a nice quarter horse that has been trained and knows what he's doing."

"You're knowledgeable about horses all of a sudden."

"We livestock owners know a bit," she said audaciously.

He smiled as a surge of longing swept through him like a tidal wave. He wanted to ride again, yearned to ride. To feel a horse between his legs, to know the freedom of crossing the open land, feeling he was an equal partner with his brother in working the ranch, and not a glorified paper pusher. But he'd put that dream away, along with others, after the accident.

Didn't she know that just wishing for things didn't make them happen? Hell, the doctors had wanted more operations, offering a slim chance of more mobility. But he couldn't take the pain and false hope they tried to peddle. He'd accepted his limitations. She had to, as well.

He turned toward the house, then looked down at her. "Clint and Sally are back."

Kelly turned at the sound of the truck. Their idyllic afternoon was over.

"I guess I'll go," she said with one last look at Sam.

"Stay for dinner," he suggested.

"No. I don't think so." She stood beside him, not wanting to leave, but not wanting to share him with his brother and Sally.

"Come again," he said softly.

She flushed at the double meaning and nodded, afraid to meet his gaze.

"I'll work with Sam. I can't wait to ride in the cart. That will be such fun." She reached up to give him a quick kiss.

His hand reached around her hips and drew her up against him, pressing into her so she would know he wanted her again. He deepened the kiss and held her against him for endless time.

Kelly didn't realize she had her arms around his neck until he slowly pulled back and she felt the tug in her shoulders. His eyes were dark and mysterious, his mouth infinitely precious. She licked her moist lips and trailed her tongue along her lower lip.

He groaned and caught it with his, kissing her again.

"If you don't leave soon, I won't let you leave at all," he said, moving his lips against hers, his breath brushing over her face.

"Hey, you two, break it up. Your chaperons have arrived."

Kelly smiled shyly at Kit and turned to see Sally's beaming face.

"Thought you said you were going to show her how to hitch the cart," Sally said to Kit as she and Clint drew near.

"We did. Just finished. I was rewarding Kelly for a job well done." His eyes flashed down at her and he grinned.

"How'd it go?" Clint asked.

"He's skittish. But I think with work, he'll settle in just fine," Kit replied.

Sally looked between the two of them, as if trying to see what else might have transpired in her absence.

Kelly climbed into her car a few moments later, her face stiff with keeping a smile in place. It was a strain being around Clint and Sally when all she wanted was to be alone with Kit.

And she didn't know what to do about Kit. She had not expected to fall in love. She had no contingency plan to help her out. She'd agreed to help him just to save face at the dance. Now her gesture had exploded into far more. Yet he hadn't given any indication he felt anything toward her but gratitude for her help. And gratitude was a poor substitute for love.

For the next few days Kelly returned to the ranch to work with Sam. Kit, Clint and Sally were there on Sunday, but during the week Kit was out and Kelly worked with the pony alone.

Wednesday Sam did so well, Kelly decided to try riding. Gingerly she climbed into the cart. Gathering the reins, one in each hand, she urged him forward. Sam turned his head and looked over his shoulder as if asking what she was doing there.

"Get up," she said again, gently slapping his rump with the reins. Gingerly he picked up his feet and began walking. Kelly was delighted. She laughed aloud and looked proudly around as they circled the house. Pulling him to a stop near the kitchen door, she called for Sally.

"Oh, you're in the cart. What fun."

"Will he pull two?" Kelly asked dubiously.

"Try and see. Should." Sally climbed in beside her.

Kelly gave the command and Sam picked right up. They went around the house twice, Kelly and Sally giggling in delight. It was a lot of fun, and Kelly couldn't wait until she could go farther afield with her little pony.

"Wait until I tell Kit," she said proudly as she drew up by the back porch again.

"He knew the pony would pull the cart. You've worked well with Sam, Kelly." Sally was sincere in her praise. "Come in for some iced tea when you've put him away."

Still smiling broadly, Kelly turned the cart toward the barn. She'd unhitch Sam and park the cart out of the way. Maybe Kit would return before she left and she could tell him of the successful rides.

She pulled the pony to a stop and dropped the reins, rising to step down from the cart. With the reins slack, Sam started again, heading for the fresh hay he knew awaited.

Kelly lost her balance as the cart jerked forward, stumbled and fell, cracking her head on the side of the cart. She saw a sharp flash of light, then nothing.

Kit was hot and tired and in a hurry. He'd been tallying cattle on one of the far pastures and it had taken longer than expected. Kelly had been working Sam every afternoon and he wanted to get back before she left today. He'd missed her each day she'd been here since Sunday.

He took the last turn fast and headed for the farmhouse. Drawing up before the deck, he killed the engine just as Sally came running around the side of the house.

"Thank God you're here. Kelly's been hurt. She's still unconscious," she said breathlessly as she yanked open his door.

Fear pierced him as he swung down from the truck and hurried after Sally. As he rounded the house he saw Kelly lying in the dirt, the pony and cart still hitched standing in the shade of the barn.

"What happened?" he asked as he drew level with her. Without a thought, he released the crutches and sank beside Kelly, reaching out to brush her hair from her face, exposing the dark bruise and scraped skin. Sally handed him a damp cloth.

"I think she fell from the cart. Didn't secure the reins when she went to get out, probably. I didn't think to tell her about that and she obviously didn't know. Oh, will she be all right?"

"Did you call the doctor?" Kit asked, his hand on her throat. Her pulse was strong and steady. "How long has she been out?"

"Just a few minutes. I called Dr. Thornton right away. He's out but his service is tracking him down. Should we get her in the house?"

Before Kit could ask how Sally planned to accomplish such a feat, Kelly moved her head and groaned softly.

"Kelly?" He brushed her cheeks with the back of his fingers.

"Kelly, wake up. Tell us how you are?"

"My head hurts, for one thing," she said crossly, her eyes still closed. "Kit?" She opened her lids a slit, wincing at the bright sunlight.

"Yes, honey. We think you fell from the cart and cracked your head. Can you see all right?"

"The light hurts my eyes. But there's only one of you. Thank God. The world couldn't handle two of you."

"You'll be fine," he said wryly. "Your mouth hasn't suffered a bit." Relief coursed through him.

"What happened?"

Nine

"**Y**ou went to lesson C without passing lesson B first," Kit said, turning the wet cloth and pressing it against her forehead. "How're you doing?"

"Umm, that feels good. Give me a couple of aspirins and I'll feel better."

"We'll wait to hear what the doctor says. How many fingers do you see?"

"I see four, two up and two down tucked under your thumb. I'm fine, really. Just a hard knock, but I'm tough."

"Yes, so tough you almost killed yourself. Just rest here a minute. Then maybe Sally can help you into the house." Damn, he was so helpless he couldn't even help her up, much less carry her into a bed where she belonged. And she was too heavy for Sally to manage.

"There's the phone. I'll get it." Sally sprinted to the back door, and the screen slammed behind her. The shrill ring of the phone was abruptly silenced.

Kit saw a movement in the distance and raised his head, narrowing his gaze. It was one of the men who worked for him, Pete.

Kit roared his name and the cowboy changed his horse's direction and headed straight for the yard at a gallop. In only a minute he swung down from his horse, tying him to the rail of the fence.

"What happened, boss?" He hurried over, his eyes on Kelly.

"She took a spill. Can you get her into the house? Put her in my bed."

"Sure thing." Pete reached out and grabbed Kit's crutches with one hand, held his other out to the boss without a word. Kit took it and was standing in a second.

"Just you relax, miss. I won't drop you." Pete knelt and picked Kelly up, straightening slowly and turning toward the house.

Kit reached the door first and opened it, holding it as Pete carried Kelly inside. She'd put her arm around his shoulder and rested her head against him. Kit's face tightened at the sight, but there wasn't a damn thing he could do about. He couldn't have brought her into the house. Hell, if it had been left to him she'd still be lying in the dirt in the yard.

Sally was talking on the phone when Kit entered. He moved to stand beside her, listening to her side of the conversation.

"Well?" he asked as she hung up.

"Doc said we should watch her closely for concussion but he can't get out here until later. If we see any change for the worse, we're to bring her to the hospital. Otherwise he'll be out this evening to see her. We're to keep her quiet and lying down."

Pete came back into the kitchen. "All set, boss. You okay?"

"Yeah, thanks, Pete. What were you doing this way?"

"The fool horse threw a shoe. I was coming in to fix it and head back out."

"Good timing," was all Kit said as he headed toward his room.

Kelly was lying on the bed and for a moment Kit's body tightened in memory of last weekend when they'd been on his bed together. He moved slowly closer. Her eyes were closed, the skin was scraped and bleeding slightly and a dark bruise was already forming over her left eye.

"Kelly?"

Her eyes opened and he could see the pain in their depths.

"We'll fix up your head. Dr. Thornton will be out later to check you out. He thinks you'll be fine. Anything else hurt besides your head?"

"My shoulder and hip. Where I landed, I guess. How's Sam?"

"Fine. We'll get him unhitched in a little while. I wanted to see you first."

Sally came in with a bowl of warm water, a cloth, some antiseptic cream and bandages. She smiled at Kelly and began to sponge off the scrape. Kelly closed her eyes as Sally cleaned the abrasion. God, her head hurt!

Kit leaned heavily on his crutches and gazed bitterly down at the woman in his bed. He hadn't hated his condition as much since the early days. He felt so helpless. What kind of woman would want a man who couldn't help her if she was injured? A man who could barely take care of himself, much less anyone else. If there'd been any doubt before, this cinched it. They had no future together. He would never tie her to a cripple.

Abruptly he turned and left the room.

Kelly endured Sally's ministrations quietly, though her head pounded. Taking two aspirins, she lay back and tried to sleep, afraid to move an inch lest the pain roar through her head again.

She felt like such an idiot. She should have thought about tying the pony's reins, or at least holding them as she got down. Of course he'd move. Kit was probably very glad their supposed romance was only a charade. He was used to competent people who could handle themselves around livestock, not ignorant ones who couldn't get out of a pony cart without falling. She wished she could go home. Hide in her room until she felt better. She wished he'd stayed and talked to her. Maybe even kissed her. Fretfully she tried to get comfortable.

Finally she drifted into a light sleep.

The doctor came after dinner and pronounced a slight concussion, recommending bed rest for a couple of days.

"I can't stay here. This is Kit's bed. Where would he sleep?" she asked Sally, who had stayed with her while the doctor was there.

"He can sleep on the sofa," Kit said from the door. "How is she, Doctor?"

"Be fine in a couple of days. But I recommend complete bed rest until then."

"I can go home," Kelly said.

"No." Kit didn't even look at her. He was talking to the doctor. "She can stay here. The sofa in the den is long enough for me to sleep on a couple of nights. Sally can see to her meals and things."

"Kit..."

"I think he's right, Kelly. You need someone to get you something to eat, and it won't be any extra trouble for us to look after you," Sally said earnestly.

"Of course it is."

She should be arguing more forcefully, but her head was pounding, her shoulder aching and her hip throbbing. All she wanted to do was escape the aches that racked her. She wasn't up to arguing.

"Here, some painkillers. Take two now, and tomorrow as you need them. I think you'll be fine within a day or two." The doctor gave her a packet, nodded to Sally and Kit and left.

"I'll get some water so you can take them now," Sally said, following behind the doctor.

Kit came into the room, up to the side of the bed.

"Don't fret, honey. It'll just make your headache worse."

"I don't want you to sleep on the sofa," she murmured fretfully.

"I've slept in worse places. Though I'd rather be sleeping there with you," he said softly, one eye on the door for Sally's return.

She opened her eyes and smiled slowly. "Sorry, cowboy, not tonight. I have a headache."

He chuckled and reached out to thread the fingers of his hand through hers, squeezing slightly, holding her smaller hand in his. "God, you scared me," he said softly, his thumb tracing the soft skin on the back of her hand, his dark blue eyes staring down into hers.

"Sorry," she said slowly. Despite the headache and aches and bruises elsewhere, she was conscious of the tingling in her hand and arm from his touch. She wanted him to kiss her, chase away the pain and make her forget how dumb she'd been.

"Oops, am I intruding?" Sally asked, pausing in the doorway, her eyes on their linked hands.

"Yes, but come in anyway. She needs the pain pills." Kit stepped back and waited while Sally helped Kelly take two pills. She set the rest of the pills and water on the bedside table.

"Need anything else?" Sally asked.

"No, thanks for everything." Kelly's voice was tired.

"Good night, then." Sally threw a saucy glance at Kit and left the room, pulling the door shut behind her.

Kit smiled grimly. Apparently their pretense was working with his sister-in-law. It was working with everyone, including himself.

Kelly opened her eyes and looked at him. "I shouldn't be taking your bed."

"Don't worry about it, honey, just get better." He leaned over and brushed his lips against her forehead, near the bandage. "See you later."

Kit worked in the office all evening, trying to keep his mind occupied, trying to forget the sight of Kelly lying in the dust, with him helpless to move her. But the image reappeared and reappeared. If it hadn't been for Pete, she might have had to lie there for hours.

His hand tightened into a fist and he stared out into the dark night sky. He'd known since the accident that he couldn't expect to have a normal life. First the bull, then Althea had made sure of that. But for the past few days he'd almost let himself think about it, almost believed it would be possible.

That had to stop. It was obvious it wouldn't work. It wouldn't be fair to Kelly. Or himself.

Even as he said it, he wanted to deny it. She'd felt so good in his arms. Her body had been so soft and feminine, her loving so tempestuous. He ached in sudden longing and desire, wanting to hold her, kiss her, love her just one more time.

He heard Clint and Sally go to bed. For a moment jealousy flashed through him at their happiness. What a bastard he was to resent his brother's happiness. He'd known the risks of the rodeo. He'd thrived on the danger and hair-raising chances. Only somehow he'd never truly thought he'd be injured.

Or what the full extent of that injury would entail. It was more than just a useless right leg. It meant he was dependent on his brother and wife, unable to do the kinds of things he had always loved. It meant he couldn't offer a woman any kind of marriage that would appeal to her. The years stretched out dismally before him. Long and endless and lonely.

The house grew quiet around him. The night was still and dark. Hours passed and Kit remained staring out the window at the past. Finally he switched off the lamp and rose. She was so close. It wouldn't hurt for one more night.

He opened the door to his room and shut it behind him. Slowly crossing until he was beside the bed, he sank down and eased off his boots. Lying back against the pillows fully dressed, he turned toward Kelly. He could barely see her in the faint light. She was on her back, asleep.

Slowly he reached out, pulling her onto him, nestling her head gently against his shoulder. Soothing back her hair, careful of the bandage.

"Umm. Kit?" she murmured, still half asleep.

"Shh, honey. Just sleep." His fingers gently combed through her soft waves, rubbing her head slightly, hoping to ease the pain that engulfed her.

"I love you," she said softly and drifted back to sleep.

His eyes stayed open in shock. Was she dreaming? Hell of a thing to say to a man holding her in bed. Did she mean it? What a nightmare if she did! He couldn't offer her anything. He'd have to make that clear in the morning. Let her know when she was better that they'd go back to being friends. That he'd give up their pretense. Better face Althea with the truth than give Kelly any cause to think their future could be together.

She smelled so sweet, and the feel of her in his arms was a delight. She snuggled against him as Kit held her, his hands absorbing the touch of her skin against his fingertips, the satiny texture of her hair, the warmth of her breath against his chest.

"I love you, too, darlin'. And there's not a damned thing I can do about it," he said softly.

When Kelly awoke the next morning she felt almost fit again, but a quick trip to the bathroom convinced her otherwise. She was relieved to return to bed, shakily drawing the covers over her and resting her head back against the pillows. The pounding eased immediately.

She was alone. Had she dreamed last night that Kit had come to bed with her? She tried to remember, but she had dreams about him often. Had last night just been another?

"Good morning. How do you feel?" Sally breezed in after sticking her head around the door. She brought a tray of scrambled eggs, bacon, biscuits and tea.

"Better. But my head started to swim when I used the bathroom."

"Doctor said a couple of days in bed. That means all day today."

"I should get up."

"Nonsense. Now you eat and I'll visit while you do."

Kelly sat up gingerly and put the tray on her lap. The food was delicious and she felt pampered to be served in bed. Her headache was not as strong as yesterday. Maybe it would go away soon. She'd taken two more of the pain pills earlier and they were starting to take effect.

"Kit and Clint already gone out?" she asked, trying to be casual.

"Yes. Won't be home for lunch, either. There's a lot to do on a cattle ranch, and we don't have a lot of hired help this time of year. What with inoculations, checking the fencing, the water, keeping tally of the herd, moving them from one pasture to another and all the government paperwork, it's a hard job. And you never know ahead of time what the beef will sell for."

"And you love being a part of it," Kelly said, smiling at her enthusiasm.

"I sure do. Of course, my folks do it, too, so I've known ranching all my life. I help the guys when things get hectic," Sally said.

"Have you known the Lockford men all your life?" Kelly asked, again conscious of the difference in their lives. She'd been shunted from home to home, and had no friends she'd known for years. Sally came from such a stable background. Did she appreciate it?

"Sure have. Though they are older than me. Clint said he noticed me when I was a senior in high school, but couldn't do anything about it then. I was too young." She giggled softly. "So he waited and asked me out three days after graduation. Then he waited until I tried college before asking me to marry him."

"Did you like college?"

"No. I only went two years." She sighed gently. "We were to be married that fall, but that's when Kit was so badly injured. When Clint offered to help him out on his ranch,

Clint postponed our wedding. He said he had to wait and see how much care Kit needed. He didn't want to tie me down. He was so stubborn about it, even when I told him there would never be anyone else for me."

Kelly looked at her, puzzled. "They weren't partners before?"

"No. Clint worked at his dad's place. We'd even talked about his taking over my folks' place when they get too tired of doing it. I'm an only child, you see. Then the accident happened. I worried for a long time that we wouldn't get married. But we finally did and things have worked out great."

"And does Kit take a lot of care?" Kelly asked carefully.

"None. I cook the meals, but he could if he wanted. He can do anything he wants, I think."

"Me, too." Kelly finished the last of her tea and gently replaced her cup. "In fact, I told him I think he should try riding again."

Sally looked surprised. "Oh, Kelly, I don't think he can do that."

"He won't know if he doesn't try. He misses it so much. He's not happy."

"You wouldn't be either, Kelly, if you'd lost your livelihood and the woman you loved," Sally explained.

Kelly kept quiet about Althea, knowing Sally was her friend. But she wished she could let her know how despicable she thought the other woman was, how awful her treatment of Kit had been when he'd been in the hospital.

Instead, she shrugged. "So maybe he should find another woman to love."

Sally looked at her for a long time. "I don't know if he can. Love a woman, I mean. Physically, I mean."

Kelly met her gaze. "Yes, he can," she said, her eyes steady.

"Well, maybe, but riding's different."

"He told me the doctors said he might never walk, yet he's done that."

"With crutches," Sally clarified.

Kelly shrugged. "So, he's still mobile."

"They also said there was a chance he'd have even more mobility if he had another operation, but he won't have it. I think he's gone as far as he can," Sally said.

"What operation?"

Sally shook her head. "I don't know all about it. Clint just told me one night that Kit was adamant about refusing any more surgery. I think he's resigned himself to what he has now."

Kelly was thoughtful. Another operation might make a difference, and Kit wasn't taking the risk? It didn't sound like him. Was there more to it than Sally knew? Hadn't Molly said something about further operations? Why hadn't Kit mentioned it to her?

Sally's eyes dropped to the empty plate on Kelly's tray. "I'll clear that away for you." She took the tray and left the room, her face troubled. Kelly leaned back and scooted down in the bed, thinking about the situation at the ranch. Did Sally and Clint ever want their own place? Were they content to live with Kit forever? Replete from breakfast and with the pills easing the throbbing in her body, she drifted back to sleep.

By afternoon she was bored. She slept as much as she could, wondering if she'd be able to sleep tonight. She'd scanned all the magazines Sally had brought her with lunch, finding farm magazines not quite her thing. She wished she had the mystery she'd started a couple of days ago, or her sketch pad. Stirring restlessly on the bed, she straightened the covers and glanced out the window.

The rolling, grass-covered hills hadn't changed since the last time she'd looked. Nothing moved in the wide expanse. Even the grass was still in the afternoon sun. No air stirred, no birds trilled. The timeless tranquillity of the land was undisturbed.

"Kelly, up for company?" Sally smiled at her in the doorway.

"Delighted, but I shouldn't take up your time. I ought to be at home," Kelly murmured.

"We went through that already. You're not a bit of trouble. And there'd be no one at your place to help you."

"Molly Benson," Kelly countered.

"She's too old to be traipsing up and down your steps. Truth to be told, I'm glad of the company." Sally perched on the chair near the bed and smiled at her guest. "It gets a little lonely here during the days. I like it better when I'm helping out on the range. At least I get to spend the day with Clint then."

"I'll be fine in a couple of days," Kelly murmured, feeling the tension building behind her forehead. Her head was beginning to ache again, just when she thought she was getting better.

"How about some iced tea?" Sally asked brightly, hopping up. She was back in only minutes. "Is everything all right?" she asked, setting down the tray of tea and handing Kelly a frosty glass.

"Sure, my head aches but I'll take another pill. Tell me about the expansion plans Kit and Clint were discussing the other evening."

With a happy nod, Sally began chatting about ranch issues, mutual friends and the Lockford plans for the future. Carefully explaining who people were, and some of the ranching terms she used, Sally made sure Kelly understood everything.

Kelly knew nothing of ranching or livestock. She listened avidly as Sally talked, soaking in everything she said. She delighted in the stories about the families in the area. She had no family of her own and longed for one. At one point Kelly wondered how Sally saw her. A nobody from the city coming in and trying to fit into the small community?

Sure, she had no family, but she wasn't exactly a nobody. She had lots of great friends and had built a satisfactory career all by herself. With talent alone. Maybe she should remember that and not long so much for the family she didn't have.

Just then the screen door slammed.

"Sally?" Kit's voice called.

"I'm in with Kelly," she called back.

"How're you feeling, Kelly?" Kit asked, appearing in the doorway. Moving to the far side of the bed, he leaned against his crutches and stared down at her, taking in the paleness of her skin, the dark bruise showing more clearly today than before.

"Better," she said, meeting his eyes for a second before sliding hers away. She tingled all over from his caring look.

"Clint back?" Sally asked, standing.

"Yes, he's in the barn."

She smiled and with a murmur about seeing them later took off to find her husband.

Kit waited until she'd left, then reached out and took Kelly's chin, turning her to face him again.

"How do you really feel?" he asked quietly.

"Like hell. My head keeps pounding, even with the pills. My hip is sore if I roll on it. How's the pony?"

"Sadder than usual," he said, his eyes dancing.

She made a face, then winced as the scrape on her forehead pulled. "Listen to me, Kit Lockford. I'm wounded. I don't need your mocking ways in my face now. I know you don't think the pony can look sad—"

"Oh, sweetheart, of course he is sad. He realized he's the reason he can't see you for a few days and his little black head is drooping."

She giggled softly. "Don't make fun of me."

His hand smoothed back her hair, tangling gently with the waves and combing through the soft tresses as he gazed down at her. "Maybe I'll wait until you're feeling better," he conceded.

She smiled up at him, delighting in the feel of his fingers in her hair, reveling in the shimmering excitement that built when she was near him. She was lost gazing into his warm eyes and wondered if she'd ever get tired of being with him. If she'd ever get over longing to spend every moment of her day with him.

"Kit, did you sleep in here last night?" she asked at last.

He smiled and nodded. "But I left before Clint got up."

"I thought I had dreamed it, but wasn't sure."

"Do you have a lot of dreams about me?" he asked whimsically.

She went still, unwilling to admit it, yet curious if he ever dreamed of her. "Some," she said slowly.

He sat on the bed, placed the crutches against the wall and leaned back, threading his fingers through hers and looking down at her as she lay against the pillows. "Tell me what they're about," he invited in a soft, sexy drawl.

It was like fine wine, intoxicating every cell in her body. She couldn't draw her eyes away; she was caught in the snare of his gaze. Heat stole into her cheeks and her heart tripped faster at his look. She couldn't reveal how she dreamed about him, how erotic those dreams were. But he was waiting for her to speak.

Saying the first thing that came to mind, she did. "Why didn't you tell me there is another operation that might help?"

He withdrew. Shut down, put up walls. Kelly was startled. She hadn't expected it. He even pulled his hand away. Looking out across the golden hills, he said nothing, his expression remote and closed. She shivered, almost wishing she hadn't asked. But if there was a chance to improve, why hadn't he taken it?

"Kit?" she prodded softly when he remained stubbornly silent.

He flicked her a glance, his eyes cold and almost defeated. He stared at her for a long moment, but Kelly felt as if he was staring right through her.

Finally he looked away and replied to her question. "I didn't tell you because I didn't feel it was any of your business."

She felt as if he'd struck her. Struggling a little, she pulled up on her elbow and glared at him. "Fine, you're probably right. It's not. Sorry I asked."

"Who told you, Sally?"

"She mentioned something today. Molly Benson mentioned something a few weeks ago. I didn't know it was a deep dark secret. And excuse me for prying." She was hurt. She thought they were at least friends who could discuss things.

"It's not a deep dark secret. Hell, it's not even a small secret. It was a possibility, that's all. Some experimental process at Stanford Medical Center. I chose not to try." His voice was void of all expression.

"Why?"

He was silent for another long moment.

"Comes from being a coward, I guess."

Ten

The words resounded in her head like a thunderclap. She sat up suddenly and stared at him. "Coward!" Clasping her hands to her head she tried to hold it on. It felt as if it would explode. Taking a deep breath she got the pain under control. He glanced at her, then away again.

"Dammit, Kit Lockford, you're nuts, do you know that? You are the last person in this world I'd associate with being a coward!"

"Yeah, well, fat lot you know. I refused any more operations. I was so tired of all the pain I just couldn't face another round," he said bitterly.

"That doesn't make you a coward. Oh, Kit, that's so understandable."

"Right. Explain that to everyone who thinks I should try for more. Have the operation, see what it can do. Never mind the pain, it'll fade and maybe you'll walk better," he snarled in repetition of all the platitudes his friends and family had spouted.

"Would it make you walk better?" she asked softly.

"There's no guarantee. Maybe. The only guarantee is there'd be more time in the hospital, more tubes, shots, searing pain. And for what? *Maybe* I'll walk better, not perfectly, never that. Just *maybe better.* But I couldn't stand the thought of all that pain for a maybe."

She stared at him, the throbbing in her head almost causing tears. If this rough rodeo cowboy who routinely experienced pain and discomfort riding the broncs and falling off bulls thought the pain from surgery was unbearable, it must be. He was not a man to flinch at the slightest thing.

His jaw was clenched, his hands balled into fists resting on his thighs. Kelly's heart melted and she lowered her hands to reach out to cover his.

"Tell me about it," she said gently, her fingers kneading the back of his fist, trying to soothe, to reach through the barrier he'd erected so quickly, to understand why he resisted.

"No."

She sighed and lay back on the pillows, drawing the covers up, suddenly conscious of the light cotton robe she wore over her gown. Both lent to her by Sally. Not that there was anything he hadn't already seen, hadn't already touched with his hands and his mouth. But she needed to protect herself. She was feeling fragile right now.

He looked down at her.

"I didn't mean to pry. I'm sure you have valid reasons for your decisions," Kelly said slowly, tracing the patterns of the coverlet, her eyes following her finger.

"I do, and they don't concern you."

"They would concern anyone that loves you," she said softly, eyes still on her fingers.

"As you do," Kit said gently, his eyes studying her averted face, waiting to see her reaction. Had she meant him to hear her declaration last night?

She nodded slowly. "As I do." Her voice was so quiet he scarcely heard her, only saw her lips move.

"Why?"

She grinned and faced him, her look amused. "Why? God, find a mirror. You are one gorgeous dude, sexy as hell, and have enough determination and courage, yes, *courage*, to satisfy four lifetimes. You're cocky and brash, but I think it's a cover-up for the kindness and genuine interest you have in your ranch, your family and your friends."

"Hell, you make me sound like some kind of damned saint."

She giggled. "Oh, no. Never that." Her eyes skimmed over him, lingering on his broad shoulders, his chest, the masculine bulge of his jeans. "Never that," she murmured again.

Kit suddenly felt like a million dollars. Like a whole man again. His body tightened in response to her sweeping gaze, and he could feel the tension thinking about the operation begin to fade. He started to grow hard under her eyes. He longed to lift some of her silky hair and run it through his fingers, feel the soft texture, smell her sweet scent. He longed to kiss her hot mouth and lose himself in her hotter body. Would he ever get over the craving for her?

But the reality of the situation swept through him. He wasn't a whole man. It was late afternoon and there were others in the house. Kelly had just been injured.

And he couldn't afford to let himself love her.

"How's your head?"

She tilted her head as she looked up at him. "Changing the subject, huh? I'm better. I'm on aspirin now. I should be able to go home tomorrow."

"It didn't look like it a moment ago. Don't push it." He eased himself down on the bed until he was lying beside her, his head on the pillow. "There's no rush to go home."

"There's no point in staying here." She tried to keep the disappointment from her voice at his lack of response to her declaration of love. He must have heard her last night. It hadn't been a dream, had it? Or was she so obvious in her feelings?

"Why did you sleep with me last night?" she asked, resting back against the pillows.

"Couldn't resist. I wanted to make sure you were okay. I waited until Clint and Sally were asleep, slipped out early this morning."

"Are you going to again tonight?" She held her breath.

"Do you want me to?" His hand involuntarily captured her head, his fingers warm and strong against her, rubbing gently to ease her headache.

She nodded, letting go.

"We'll see."

Afraid he'd leave, Kelly searched around for a topic of conversation that would keep him with her for a while longer. "What did you do today? Sally's been telling me something about ranching."

"What do you want to know? Today? I drove out along the northern boundary, checked out the portion of the herd grazing there. We've got a large percentage of the herd in that area. Wanted to make sure we didn't have any breaks in the fence, nor any cattle down."

"Can you drive your truck all over?"

"Just about."

"Could you ride a horse?"

He looked at her, his eyes growing hard. "Would you stop with that."

She shook her head. "Not unless you try."

"Why is it important to you whether or not I ride again?"

"Because I think it's important to you and that makes it important to me."

He ran his hands through his hair in exasperation, rolling over to his back. "Drop it, Kelly." His tone brooked no argument.

"Maybe I'll give a party when I'm better," she said, abruptly changing the subject.

He looked at her in surprise. "A party, what for?"

"Do you like parties?"

He shrugged. "Haven't gone to many the last few years. I used to party all the time—isn't that what the gossips in town say?"

"I can't quite reconcile that image with this successful ranch. I think you put on a good show, but you are a hard worker and I don't know why you don't let others know that. Is it some kind of macho cowboy thing?"

"Sometimes I think if I was a banker, you'd never look at me twice. Are you in love with the cowboy mystique?"

"No. I know who I'm in love with. Are you in love with me?"

He looked away, refusing to answer. He didn't have to. His silence let her know.

She sighed gently and started tracing the pattern on the coverlet again, her eyes blurring a little from the tears that filled them. Tears she refused to let fall. She opened her mouth a little, blinking her eyes quickly, trying to erase all trace of her distress. She would not use those kinds of tricks. If he loved her it would be wonderful, but her love wasn't based on reciprocity. She loved him regardless.

"Why a party?" he asked at long last.

"Just because I don't have any family doesn't mean I haven't accomplished anything with my life, or that I don't have a lot of good friends," Kelly said slowly.

He looked back at her, wondering where she had come up with that. Where was she leading?

"No one ever said that."

"Maybe not, but you don't know that's not what people are thinking. I want to have some of my old long-time friends out. Let my new friends meet them. Share some of my new life with my old friends. It'll be a house party that I could have for a whole weekend. What do you think?"

"Do you miss the city?"

"No. But I miss my friends." And I think I want to show off to you, show you what I've done with my life so far. Maybe then you'll forget Althea and look at me.

"Sounds nice."

"Do you think people I've met here would come?"

"Sure."

"I could have a barbecue, maybe ask the Soames sisters to help out with the food, like Sally did. Would some of your ranch hands do the meat?"

He nodded.

She smiled and went on, planning as she talked.

"I could have a wooden platform built in the backyard for dancing. Get some music."

"Going all out, I see."

"Umm. Would you dance with me?"

"What? For God's sake, Kelly, I can't even walk. How the hell do you think I can dance? I'm not capable. I'm a cripple. Disabled. Stop looking at everything like determination alone can overcome it."

She stared back at him, holding his gaze with her own.

"Not fast dancing. But slow dancing, where people mostly stand still and rub their bodies against each other. I'd like that," she said softly, painting a seductive picture in his mind.

"I'd like that part, too, but not standing up, lying down." He leaned over her, putting his hands on either side of her head and lowering his mouth to hers.

"I'd like it right now, but the timing stinks."

She smiled and quickly moistened her lips, her eyes glued to his, her love shining from her depths.

"Maybe later."

"Umm." He sank the last few inches and closed over her with a burning need that surprised him. Her lips opened slowly, drawing out the moment, extending the anticipation slightly. But when his tongue slowly pushed through the barrier of her teeth, she met him and slowly danced through a mating ritual that was both exciting and erotic.

"Kit, you want to go over those figures before dinner?" Clint called from down the hall.

With a sigh Kit kissed her again, quickly, hard on her mouth, and sat up.

"Later?" Kelly whispered.

Without a word he left.

Kelly insisted on joining them for dinner. She remained in Sally's borrowed gown and robe, but showered and brushed her hair until it floated around her face in a soft blond cloud. The white bandage over her scrape stood in stark relief to the tan she'd acquired recently, the bruise a purple patch of color.

"I'll return home in the morning," she said as they began the meal.

"So soon? Are you feeling up to it?" Sally was concerned.

"Yes. My headache's almost gone." Involuntarily her eyes flicked to Kit's. He met her gaze, devilish light dancing in his. She flushed, looking down at her plate. Was he remembering last night when she'd said she had a headache? Did he think she was now issuing an invitation? Was he wrong?

"Besides, Kit wants his room back."

"I never said that," he replied.

"No, but it can't be comfortable sleeping on a couch."

"I was fine last night."

It was all Kelly could do to keep a straight face. Sure, he'd been in his own bed. Why wouldn't he be fine?

"I appreciate you all taking care of me."

"You aren't any trouble. And it's nice to have someone else around who doesn't talk cattle or beef prices all the time," Sally said.

"Surely not all the time?" Kelly asked, wide-eyed.

"No," Kit said.

"Yes," Sally said.

"Let's make a pact that tonight we don't talk about beef, cattle or ranches," Kelly suggested, looking back and forth between Clint and Kit, the challenge clear in her eyes.

"Fine."

"Okay with me."

"They'll never be able to make it," Sally predicted.

The evening turned out to be fun. The topic of conversation ranged from current movies, to books, to various places to see in California that none of them had ever visited. They discussed their various tastes in music, Clint and Kit predictably liking country and western, but unexpectedly liking some classical, as well. Kelly told them about being on the committee for the San Francisco Symphony and there were lots of questions about that.

They moved to the deck after dinner, enjoying the balmy evening and the quiet sounds of the ranch settling down. They kept the lively conversation going until they got into politics. When Clint and Kit started arguing opposing positions on some proposed legislation, Kelly quickly changed the subject.

"I'm thinking of giving a party. Did Kit tell you?"

Sally was delighted and offered to help when she heard Kelly's ambitious plans.

"Sounds very sophisticated. Are we to dress up?"

"I hadn't thought of that. What do you think?" Kelly asked.

"Yes. We get to so rarely out here."

"Does that mean suits?" Clint asked, horrified.

"Not for the guys," Sally said. "But I'd love a pretty party dress, not the same old one I wear to church most Sundays."

"I thought jeans," Kit said.

"Oh, you men. It won't kill you to dress up a little for one night. Oh, Kelly, it'll be great. I can't wait to meet your friends from San Francisco. Will they think us very provincial, do you think?"

"I think they'll like my new friends as much as I hope you will like them."

"We'll provide some of the meat," Kit said. "But it won't be pork."

"Won't be chicken, either," Clint added.

"What will it be?" Sally asked, starting to catch on.

"Can't say." Kit smiled at her, then Kelly.

"Very good. See, Sally, they can go all night without talking about the B word."

The gentle laughter they all shared was like fine wine to Kelly. It filled her senses, enchanted her and made her long for more. She ached to belong to a family like this. To be a part of it forever, not just for an evening.

She ached to belong to Kit, she thought as her eyes sought his. To share her life with him until they were both old and gray. Yet he'd never even hinted at such a thing. How did he feel about her? Truly feel about her?

Kelly was the first to suggest bed. Her head ached and she was tired. She said good-night and went off to Kit's room, hoping he'd come later as he'd promised.

Truly tired, she fell asleep once she lay down.

"Kelly?" Kit's soft voice broke through her sleep, drifted across her senses and brought her slowly awake.

"Umm?" She turned, seeking him. He was stretched out beside her, beneath the covers. She rolled over, moving closer, resting her head on his chest. His bare chest.

Her eyes opened.

"Kit?" She snuggled closer, letting her hand brush the crisp hair covering his chest, drifting down to see if he was wearing anything. When she reached the scars, she knew he wasn't.

"Are you awake?" His arms came around her, drawing her up against the long, hot length of him.

"I am now. How late is it?"

"After midnight."

"I tried to stay awake," she said, rubbing her fingers over his scars lightly, feeling his muscles contract at her touch.

His hands roamed over her back, down her spine, tracing the hollow at her lower back, causing waves of shimmering electricity. Back up, kneading the muscles gently, tracing her spine again.

She shivered and moved closer, feeling him draw her gown up, baring her back. His calluses were rough against her skin, but it only enhanced the sensations his touch brought, and she shivered again in delight. His hands moved against her, up and down, hypnotically, mesmerizing, arousing. When he cupped her bottom, he pulled her up a little higher, allowing his fingers access to the dark, moist heat of her.

"You're already ready," he said in wonder.

She couldn't answer, couldn't talk at all, only feel the ripples of pleasure starting to build with the movement of his fingers. She slid one knee over his thigh, opening her legs for his hands, nudging his arousal with her soft leg.

Taking advantage of the gesture, his hands moved against her, fingers slipping in, testing her, teasing her, stroking her.

Heat and desire built rapidly in Kelly. She moved her hips, seeking more, seeking escape, seeking pleasure. One of his large hands held her still, the other continuing its massage, building up the tension, building up the hunger she couldn't deny.

"Oh, Kit, please!" She jerked against his hand, her hips seeking to move, his hand holding her against it.

"Not yet, honey. Let it build."

"It's already intense," she gasped. She was dying.

"Let it build." His hand never stopped. His clever fingers fondled her until she was mindless with longing and yearnings.

Her hands raked his chest, tangling in the hair, pulling, rubbing his nipples, seeking to give him the same fiery hunger he built so high in her.

When she moved lower and encircled him, he drew in a deep breath. But his hand never stopped, and she was about to explode.

She squeezed gently, moving up and down over the hard, heavy weight of him.

"Uh-uh, honey. Don't do that."

"Stop me," she said, breathing hard, her body a quivering mass of burning need and cravings. He would drive her mad. If she could do it to him, so much the better.

He eased her onto her back, coming between her wide-spread thighs, his hand still intent on its mission. Kelly arched up against him.

"Please! Kit, I'm going to explode!"

"Explode with me, honey." His mouth covered one breast and suckled the hard tip, drawing it deep into his mouth, inflaming it with his hot tongue. The flame flashed from her nipple to the fiery core deep within her, threatening to engulf her.

Just when she thought she couldn't contain herself anymore, he thrust into her. Lying against her softness, Kit raised himself up on his elbows, his breath coursing over her face, over her cheeks, in gulps. He wasn't as immune as she'd thought.

Kelly raised up to take all of him. When he withdrew, she denied it, tried to stop it, but he only plunged down into her hard as ever. Again. Kelly reached up to match his rhythm, her own body throbbing with need.

She couldn't hold back her cries as she reached the summit. His mouth covered hers, trying to absorb them into his own as she cried out in ecstasy as wave after wave of rapture swept through her. She could feel it throughout her entire body, from the fiery core at her center to her tingling fingers and toes. It went on and on and on. She thought she would never stop. She was aware only of the intense pleasure that coursed through her, and the even hotter heat of Kit as he went with her.

Collapsing in exhaustion, Kelly couldn't move. She'd never felt such intense delight and pleasure in her whole life! Never imagined it could exist. Her muscles continued to convulse around him, contract, release, contract.

He lay on her, supporting some of his weight on his elbows, but allowing the length of his body to rest against hers. Kelly could feel every inch of him, feel him and relished the touch. His heat burned into her as hers burned into his. She could scarcely breathe. She wondered if she'd lose consciousness, or gradually return to earth.

Soon she could breathe normally, but she had no energy. She couldn't even lift her eyelids. Repletion had never been so deep.

He still filled her, and her muscles contracted around him again. When he moved his hand between them, she was sharp with instant awareness.

"No," she mumbled. But he ignored her and in only seconds the fiery desire was building again. It couldn't be, but it was. His hand was magic. It brought her to another high, and she climaxed again, straining against his body, pushing and twisting, struggling to reach the glorious peak.

Molten lava spread through her. Heat, scalding and torrid, flushed every nerve ending, every fiber of her being. Her heart pounded, her breathing stopped and she gave way to the glorious rapture that claimed her again.

When she could breathe again she was going to talk to this man. If she lived that long.

She was asleep before he withdrew from her.

When Kelly awoke, she had no idea as to the time. Was it near dawn? Would Kit be leaving soon? She was held in his arms, her back against his chest, her legs entwined with his. His hand was on her breast, heavy in sleep.

She smiled. She liked sleeping with him. Wished they could do it every night. Wake up together every morning.

Suddenly his hand tightened.

"Are you awake?" she whispered.

"Umm. You?"

"Yes." She shifted around on her back, tried to see him in the dark. "I never knew my body could feel that," she whispered. "It was the most wonderful thing I ever knew."

"Me, too." He kissed her cheek, licking the soft texture of her skin. Moving to kiss her mouth gently.

Kelly was quiet for a long time, thinking about the night, about how remarkable everything had been. Then a shadow crossed her happiness.

"Did you make love to Althea like that?" she asked softly.

Kit went rigid. He held himself stiff for a long moment, then moved across the bed to snap on the light.

Kelly closed her eyes at the sudden brightness, but he captured her face between his hard hands, his palms on her jaw, his fingers threaded in her hair. He turned her to face him and she slowly opened her eyes.

He was mad. She could have felt that from his hard grip, but the blazing anger in his eyes told her she'd gone too far.

"Kelly, I'm only going to tell you this once and I don't want you to ever bring it up again. All right?"

She tried to nod her head, but his hands held her so tightly she couldn't move. But he must have felt her attempt. She wished she'd kept her mouth shut. She didn't think she was going to like what he told her.

"You know I was wild when I was younger. You've been told that by anyone who knows me. Right?"

She tried to nod again.

"Hell, I've slept with so many women I can't count them all. Groupies follow winners at rodeos. The adrenaline rush during the competition stays with you and after the shows, I'd take any willing woman. Almost all the guys did. It meant nothing but a release after the stress of the show."

She nodded again, his grip loosening slightly, but still he held her head close to his, his palms hard against her jaw.

"But I've only made love a few times. To Althea and to you. But what I felt with Althea can't begin to compare to what I feel with you, Kelly. She was almost as wild as I was, wanting the sex for a release. And it was sex, pure and simple. Or not so simple, maybe. But I didn't feel with her what I feel with you. With you it's hot and exciting and never enough. Yet I feel complete, as if more than our bodies touch, communicate. You are not a substitute for anyone or anything when you're in my arms. I have never felt so strongly about anything."

She blinked, wanting to say something, but not knowing what to say. Her heart swelled with love for him and she longed to take him in her arms and share that love with him.

"The past is over, gone, finished. It won't ever be repeated. I wish tonight that I hadn't done everything I have done, but know I can't change a thing. I have to live with it and you will, too. But I don't want it discussed again. Is that clear?"

She nodded. "I love you, Kit," she said softly, her eyes never leaving his.

"Hell, I wish you didn't," he groaned, lowering his mouth to hers.

When she could speak again, she tugged at his wrists and he raised his head.

"Maybe you love me, too. Maybe that's why the sex is different," she said hopefully, aching for it to be true.

"No, I don't. I can't. Don't you understand I have nothing to give a woman?"

"I can't believe you said that. You have more than enough to give any woman. More than enough for me!"

"You're setting yourself up for a truckload of heartbreak if you set your sights on me, honey."

Kelly didn't answer. She was not going to argue about it and set his back up again. She wanted to share her love for him, not make him withdraw. Reaching up, she pulled his head back down and kissed him with all the love she had.

He turned off the light and gathered her closer as they settled down to sleep the rest of the night.

"Kit," she whispered after a long time.

"Now what?" He didn't sound asleep.

"After the accident, were you told you couldn't make love again?"

"No."

"Why didn't you before me?"

"Never had the urge."

She thought carefully how she should word the next part.

"Was it hard to learn to walk?"

"Yes. Not that they said I couldn't. But I had no intention of spending my life in a wheelchair."

"Did they ever tell you you couldn't ride again?"

"Yes. Dammit, I can't believe you are bringing that up again. Drop it."

"If you would try one time for me, I promise never to bring it up again as long as I live. No matter what happens."

"Go to sleep, Kelly."

"Please?"

He was silent for a long time, his body stiff with tension.

"Kelly, I can't change what I am, what I can do. If you can't accept me as I am, maybe we shouldn't see each other anymore. I can't change just to please you." He held his breath. God, the thought of not seeing her again was enough to tear him apart.

She was shocked. "Kit, I don't want you to *change*. I only want you to go for all you can. It's none of my business and I'm sorry if you thought I was pushing you for more on my account. I'm perfectly satisfied with you the way you are. I love you, if you recall my mentioning it. But if you could be happier riding, why not try it? I thought I was encouraging you, not trying to change you. I'm sorry." She was almost in tears. How could he think she wanted him any different from the way he was? Granted, if a miracle happened and he could walk unaided again, she'd be delighted. But his limitations didn't matter to her one bit. If he were happier with himself, though, she thought, he might let himself love her. Riding again could do it. But riding or not, she loved him just as he was—irritable, arrogant, bossy and sexy as hell.

"I'll think about it," he said at last.

It was the most she could hope for right now. He was a man of his word. If he'd think on it, maybe it would be a small step to trying. It would be enough. Snuggling closer to him, she fell asleep with a smile on her lips.

Eleven

Kit was gone when she awoke the next morning. She stretched, wincing at the soreness of certain muscles, then smiled with remembered memories of last night. God, she loved him so much! And his lovemaking was the stuff dreams were made of.

She showered carefully and donned her clothes from a few days ago. Sally had laundered them for her and they were clean and fresh. Brushing her hair, she grimaced at the bandage. How much longer would she need it?

She found Sally in the kitchen and they chatted casually while they ate breakfast.

"I'm off as soon as I help you clean up," Kelly said, eating the last of her toast.

"No need to clean up. Not much to do and if you help, I'll have empty time on my hands. I'm sorry you got hurt, but it's been fun having you here."

"Thanks for taking care of me. I would have had a hard time at home alone." She carefully refrained from asking after Kit, hoping he'd come to tell her goodbye. But she neither saw nor heard him. Well, they had covered some serious ground in their talk last night. Kit had some thinking to do—and so did she. If he wanted to see her, he knew where to find her.

"I guess I'll wait a little while before I take the pony out again," Kelly said as Sally walked her to the car.

"We'll exercise him. And I'm sure Kit will keep working with him. He's good about doing things like that," Sally said.

"I know. Though not from his reputation. I thought he'd be reckless and incorrigible from the rumors I heard before I knew him. But he's nothing like that."

Sally smiled and nodded. "I think it's some sort of male thing. I was actually afraid of him when I met him. And very nervous about coming here when Clint and I married. He still makes me nervous. But he works hard, and until recently hasn't had a chance to play. You're good for him, Kelly."

"He's good for me. Well, thanks again. See you soon." She climbed into her car and headed for home. She wished she could have seen him before she left.

Kit had to force himself to work this morning. He glanced at his watch again. Would she have left by now? He looked up at the fence Pete and Mark were repairing, wondering what he was doing here when he longed to be with Kelly. Damn, he wished he could have stayed in bed with her until she woke up. Kissed her awake, made love to her again.

He had to stop thinking of her. He was getting obsessed with her, and he knew there was no future in that. Yet not thinking of her was easier said than done. At odd moments he'd remember her coming apart in his arms last night. He'd never made a woman reach such pleasure before. It made him feel whole again. A sudden thought popped into his mind.

"*Ah, hell,*" he said softly, closing his eyes in anguish. *He'd not used any protection.* He hadn't been able to stop long enough to get anything, hadn't even thought of it once.

She drove him mad and he reacted. Did Kelly know? He'd taken care of it before.

She had to know, if she thought about it. He felt his heart squeeze against his chest, and breathing was difficult. What a consequence. He needed to talk to her.

Tell her what? Sorry, I got caught up in the moment and didn't think of protection. Hope you're not pregnant.

What if she was? Then what?

Kit started the truck, calling to the men that he was leaving, and headed across the field. He and Clint had installed automatic gates at each crossing, so he used his remote to open the gates barring his way. Before long he reached the house.

Kelly's car was gone. She had already left. He stopped the truck and sat, gazing out over the fields. Now what? He'd have to tell her. But how? And what if she was pregnant?

A feeling of astonishment swept through him. And anticipation. He'd like to have a baby with Kelly. Have several children with her.

Was he crazy? He couldn't even marry her—how could they have children? It was one thing to have an affair with him. But she'd never tie herself to him and he wouldn't ask her to. He wouldn't ask any woman to pledge her future with him. It would be asking too much.

He climbed out of the truck and made his way to the barn, feelings at odds with his mind. Trying to ignore the warm glow that he felt when he thought of a baby growing in Kelly, of her stomach heavy with his child. Damn, he couldn't afford such thoughts. Logically they had no future together. He knew that.

He knew it as well as he knew he'd never walk normally again. As well as he knew he couldn't ride again.

Pausing near the corral where a couple of his cutting horses dozed, he leaned against the rails and watched the horses, remembering his promise to Kelly to think about riding. She was such a damned optimist. Why wouldn't she face reality? Didn't she understand the extent of his injuries? Wishing things different wouldn't make it so.

His stomach clenched with nerves and apprehension as he stared at the horses. He'd promised to think about riding. Could he possibly do it? The doctors had said he might never walk, yet he did, after a fashion. Could he ride?

He longed to feel the warmth and strength of a horse between his legs, to feel the air rush by as he moved with his mount. To go where a truck couldn't, be alone with an animal that would carry him wherever he directed, just the two of them. He yearned to know that kind of independence and freedom again. It would make him feel almost whole. He longed to feel the power between his legs, feel the same rush he felt when he rode the broncs and bulls.

He considered it. He'd promised he would and he did. The first barrier was mounting. He didn't have enough strength in his left leg to mount. The second problem would be staying on, getting his right leg in the stirrup, holding on.

Despite his best efforts, excitement began building within. He wanted to ride. He yearned to ride again. Could he? God, he was getting as bad as Kelly, thinking he could do all he used to do. Bitterness surged through him as he turned and went toward the house. He'd accepted his limitations two years ago. No use wishing for the moon at this late stage.

With her book finished it was time to start another. Kelly threw herself into plans for a new story. This time she'd write about a little city girl's adventure on a real ranch. She couldn't wait to get started.

As the week progressed, Kelly's headaches stopped. Her shoulder was no longer stiff, and the bruise on her hip was fading. Still she didn't return to the Lockford ranch. She spoke to Sally every couple of days, asking after Sam. As casually as possible each time, Kelly would ask after Clint and Kit, longing to hear how Kit was, a bit angry with him that he didn't call her or come by.

She thought about making plans for her party, but each time she sat down to pick a date and make a guest list, she soon felt distracted. It always came back to Kit. When Kelly imagined her party, she saw herself introducing Kit to her friends as the man she loved, and who loved her. But that was not to be. Finally, Kelly decided to postpone her plans for a party until she had a clearer mind, and a clearer idea of where she stood with the stubbornest, most contrary man in the world.

A week after she'd returned to town, Kelly received a call from Sally.

"I'm bored today. The guys are out and the house is cleaned. Come out and take me for a ride in the cart."

Kelly hesitated only a moment. She was a little nervous about driving the pony cart after her mishap, but knew how to avoid a repeat and was anxious to see Sam again. And Kit if she was lucky.

"When?"

"Come around two and plan to stay for dinner."

Her heart beating faster, Kelly smiled and agreed.

The afternoon turned out to be fun. She and Sally took the pony out into the flat fields surrounding the main house and took turns driving. They laughed at silly jokes and talked endlessly of ranching, books and San Francisco.

Finally it grew late and Sally said she'd have to return for dinner. Her eyes scanned the hills surrounding them as if looking for something, then she turned toward home. Kelly drove carefully and soon pulled to a stop beside the barn.

"This time I'll hold him until you get down," Sally said, climbing down and going to Sam's head.

Working together, the two women unhitched the pony and turned him loose in the main corral. Climbing up on the top rail, Sally scanned the horizon again, then patted the worn wood.

"Come on up and watch horses with me. We have a few minutes before we need to get supper."

Kelly easily joined her, balancing carefully on the slippery rail, and watched a couple of horses in the corral amble over to them curiously. Sally drew some sugar cubes from her pocket and gave half to Kelly, doling them out slowly to the greedy horses.

Kelly laughed at the touch of their soft lips against her palm, remembering how frightened she'd been that first day with Sam. Kit had held her hand that day, and even then she'd been aware of the sizzling pulse that arced between them.

Just then she heard a noise like distant thunder. She looked up. The sky was cloudless. Sally grinned and scanned the hills again.

"There, look." She pointed toward the right. Cresting the hill were the riders of the Lockford ranch. Spread out like the cavalry at a charge, they galloped across the ridge and down the sloping hill that led to the ranch house. The sound of the hooves was loud, pounding like thunder, and dust rose behind them like a following cloud.

Kelly watched, as excited as a kid at an old-fashioned Western movie, the throbbing of the horses' beat matching her heartbeat. As the men drew closer, they began to yell, a couple swept their hats off and waved them in the air, but none faltered and none slowed.

She could see Pete, riding a big brown horse. There was Mark and the other man she didn't know yet. Clint was to the side and beside him...

Kelly caught her breath, her eyes only for the tall, dark man on the sorrel horse. He was riding as hard as the others, the look of supreme satisfaction visible to her from where she sat. Tears threatened as she watched him, her heart in her throat.

Kit was riding! Riding hell-for-leather, just like some rash, reckless, brash, wild rodeo cowboy! She couldn't believe it. He was riding!

The men drew near, the cadence of the pounding hooves blurred into a dull roar at the different gaits of the separate horses. The men continued to yell, and raced to the barn, drawing up at the last moment, laughter and cheers rending the air.

Kelly turned carefully on the slippery rail and watched Kit, her eyes never leaving him as she saw him slow the horse and then walk calmly up to her.

Sitting on the rail, she was even with him. He could see the tears coursing down her cheeks, and she brushed them away, more cascading down. Her lower lip was caught in her teeth and the smile she gave almost broke his heart.

"You're riding!" she said, her voice shaky and soft. For one moment she knew she saw him as he'd been before the accident. Cocky and insolent, bold and brazen, and wild and sexy enough to draw every woman for fifty miles around. Each one of them wanting to try to contain him, be the one to conquer him.

He pushed his horse up to her, pressing into her legs. His strong arm swept around her and he pulled her before him on the saddle, turning her to face the front, drawing her back into the cradle of his legs.

"Come on." He turned the horse and walked it out of the yard. The others were still yelling, Sally laughing and Clint calling after him to return in time for dinner.

Kit waved, then urged the horse faster.

Kelly clutched his arm, leaning back into the safety of his embrace and holding on for the ride.

"I had no idea," she said, the wind in her face, her hair blowing back into his.

"You should have. You are even more determined than I. Nag, nag, nag."

She laughed and turned to see him, her heart catching at the happiness radiating from his eyes. "I knew you could."

"Maybe. I promised to consider it, at least. And when I finally did, I thought, might as well try."

"And?"

The horse was blowing hard, struggling up the incline, and Kit pulled him down into a walk, skirting the hill and following the gentle curve to the left.

"And so I decided to see if I could. I called a meeting of all the men, and Clint. Told them what I wanted and what I could do. We brainstormed ideas. The worst part is mounting. So we rigged up a lift in the barn. I need someone to help me, but only for about seven seconds."

"Seven seconds? What did you do, time it?"

"Yes. Then we devised this quick-release brace for my right leg. It holds it in the saddle, but I can release it if I need to in a hurry. After that, it was just doing it."

"I knew you could," she said again.

"Well, the first few days I wondered. I was as sore as hell. Couldn't move when I'd get down."

"But it was worth it?"

"Yeah, more than worth it."

She could hear the spark in his voice, knew he'd never expected to come back this far. Her love for him grew and a deep happiness invaded her.

"Is it dangerous?"

"No, if I fall, I'll just be stuck somewhere until Clint finds me. But you know I like living on the edge of danger."

"Great, now I'll have to start worrying about you."

"No, you don't. Nobody has to worry about me. I'm not going to fall. This gelding is one of the best-trained horses we have. I'm not going to be doing anything to put him to the test. We'll get by just fine."

She smiled and snuggled against him, her bottom wiggling against his thighs and the growing hardness she felt there. His arms tightened around her ribs, one hand splayed across her, his fingers moving in a slow, seductive dance.

"Thank you, honey, for pushing."

"You are one stubborn cowboy," she said smugly, so happy he had tried. So pleased with the result her heart swelled with delight. "So will you dance with me when I give my party?"

"Dammit, don't you ever give up?" he growled in her ear.

She giggled and shook her head. "Never."

They rode in silence for a long time, enjoying the evening, enjoying being together. Finally Kit turned the sorrel back toward the ranch. Supper would be ready soon and the horse was getting tired. And he still had to talk to Kelly about their last night together.

"Kelly," he said, wondering just how he was going to do this.

"Yes?"

"I need to talk to you."

"Okay. You've got me captive. What do you want to talk about?"

"The last night we were together."

Her heart lurched and her stomach tightened in memory. It had been fabulous, the most marvelous experience of her life. She tried to relax against him, but her body began tingling in tension and anticipation. She'd lived that night over and over each night since as she'd gone to bed. Her dreams had been full of Kit and his body and the wondrous things he'd done with her.

He felt her change, and his own body treacherously began to crave the special heat of hers. Damn, he didn't want to get hard now. He had to get through this.

"We got carried away."

"Yes." She said it dreamily.

"I didn't use anything," he said without further buildup. Damn, she wasn't helping.

Kelly was silent for a long time, wondering why exactly Kit was bringing this up. She'd realized the next morning that he'd used nothing. She'd been too caught up in her own feelings and in loving him to know that night. But the next morning she'd known.

"What do you want me to say?" she asked.

"I didn't mean for it to happen like that. But I just…" Just what, forgot everything but breathing, and that had been touch and go? Forgot any kind of prudence and gave way to his physical needs, maybe condemning them to something neither really wanted?

"I know that."

"Could you be pregnant?"

"Could be, I guess. Won't know for a while," she said slowly, the reality of the situation suddenly hitting her. Was she to repeat her mother's pattern? Is this what had happened to her mother? This overwhelming love for a man? The burning desire for his child regardless of whether they could build a life together? At least there'd be a part of him with her always.

Her mother had not expected to die young. She'd probably thought to raise her daughter, keep part of the man she loved with her when he had deserted her. Had she felt such a deep love for her father as Kelly felt for Kit?

"You're awfully calm about it," he said, the ranch house now in view. Some of the men were still in the yard. His time was running out.

"What do you want, hysterics? I don't know if I am pregnant or not. It will take a while to find out. I'm not all that regular. You certainly couldn't set a clock by me, so I just don't know. But it's too late to worry about it. If it's done, it's done."

"There are things you can do...."

She yanked on the reins, stopping the startled horse. Turning, she glared at him. *She would never have an abortion!* "Don't you worry about me or anything that's mine. I won't try to trap you into any kind of marriage. We both know you don't want to marry me. If I have a baby, fine. I'll take care of it. If not, fine, too."

"Kelly, I can't marry anyone. It's not just you. What kind of husband would I make? I couldn't even help you up when you fell. Dammit, look at it from my point of view."

"All I see when I see your point of view is a stubborn, arrogant man who is too afraid to open up the possibilities in his life. They said you couldn't walk, and you proved them wrong. Couldn't ride a horse. Well, buster, you ride better than I do and there's nothing wrong with either one of my legs. Who knows what they said about sex, but if I end up pregnant, that will blow that theory out the window."

"There's more to marriage than that," he said angrily.

"Sure there is. There's love and trust and caring. And the desire to share a life with someone through hard times and good times. But you wrap your hard times around you like a cloak and don't let anyone near you."

She swung her leg over the saddle and slid down to the uneven ground.

"Kelly..."

"I'll walk from here. I don't want to stay for dinner. I don't want to see you again until I know for sure if I'm going to have a baby or not. Then I'll let you know. And let you know what I'm going to do about it."

"Kelly!"

"And I'll tell you something else, Kit Lockford." She walked along, trying to keep a straight line to her car, but the ground was broken and she wrenched her ankle twice. Watching where she was going, she was relieved to get onto the packed ground near the house. "I will take perfect care of my baby. And when it grows up I'll tell it how its mother and father loved him into being. I'm not afraid of it, even if you are."

"Dammit, Kelly. I'm not husband material."

"Right you are, Kit, but not because of your accident." She reached her car, yanked open the door and slammed it behind her.

Starting the engine, she pulled away, refusing to look in the rearview mirror, refusing to look at Kit as she drove rapidly from the ranch.

He made her so mad she could spit! How could he think she wouldn't want his baby? Was he deaf? Hadn't she told him more than once that she loved him? Loved him just as he was. Was she fighting a losing battle? Would he never give in and admit he loved her? He had to! He couldn't have made love to her as he did that last night if he didn't love her. Surely he wouldn't have tried to ride for her if he didn't care something for her. Why couldn't he admit it?

He was brave in so many ways. Had he been too hurt to be brave in this last area? What would it take to breach his walls and pull them down?

Or was she only fooling herself? Maybe he didn't love her. Maybe he wasn't afraid to tell her, or admit it to himself. Maybe he only wanted her for sex and not for love.

She shook her head. There was more between them than that! And she was going to make Kit admit it. Somehow, some way.

Eight long days later she knew. True to her promise, she called him first thing. It was still early—he wouldn't have left the house yet. Kit answered the phone.

"Kit?" She had to make sure she didn't confuse him with Clint.

"Yes."

"I'm not pregnant." And she hung up the phone.

It was stupid to feel so sad about the situation, she tried to tell herself as she ate toast and tea for breakfast. She'd have been in a far worse situation if she had been pregnant. But at odd times during the past few days she'd thought about his baby. Thought how much she'd love it and care for it. And she knew if something ever happened to her as it had her mother, Clint and Sally would raise the child with love.

Chances were good she'd live to an old age. *And I'll have Kit's baby,* her mind played over and over. They'd have had a tie binding them for as long as their child was around. But she didn't want to bind him that way. She wanted his love to bind him to her as hers bound her to him.

The daydreams ended now. It was over.

The doorbell sounded as she was washing her breakfast dishes. She dried her hands as she went toward the front. Who would be calling this early? It was barely nine o'clock.

She opened the door and stared at him in surprise. Kit.

He looked at her and moved to enter, forcing Kelly to take a step back to let him pass.

"Are you okay?" he asked, reaching out to close the door.

She nodded.

"Come here." He leaned against the wall and waited.

Kelly hesitated a moment, then with a rush of longing stepped forward and was enfolded in his warm embrace. She felt as if she'd come home, as if she belonged. She closed her eyes, tears seeping through her lids despite her efforts to keep them contained. Resting her head on his shoulder, she hoped he wouldn't see. God, she was so disappointed.

"I'm sorry," he said softly.

Surprised, she looked up, her lashes spiky with tears.

One finger traced her damp lashes, brushing away the tears as he gazed deep into her eyes. His mouth covered hers and his kiss was gentle, soothing, comforting.

One of his crutches clattered to the floor. Kelly jumped and pulled back slightly, then leaned against him again, her head again on his shoulder. She wished she could stay in the safety of his arms forever.

His hand came up and brushed in her hair, his fingers combing the shiny tresses, soothing her, caressing her.

"It's better that you're not," he said softly, clamping down on the anguish her words had caused.

"Maybe. But I'm not getting any younger and I would like to have children." *Yours.*

"Time enough for that. You're not that old."

"No, but I need to do something before I get too old. Maybe I should take Beth up on her offer to introduce me to her cousin."

Kit went rigid. "What the hell are you talking about?"

"Well, if I want to do something about children, I have to find a man to marry. I like it here, so I should find someone from around here. Doesn't that make sense?"

She could feel the tension in him, and wondered if he had never thought of her with another man. Would that influence his thought process at all?

"Find someone for what?" His voice was ominously calm.

She pulled back a little and noticed the look on his face. Maybe it was time he started thinking things through. She didn't belong to him. He'd made that clear. Maybe it was time he understood what that meant.

"Want some coffee? I was doing dishes."

"No, I want to know what the hell you're talking about."

"Come on in the kitchen and we can discuss it while you have some coffee. Why did you come? Wasn't the phone call enough?"

"I wanted to see you." He hesitated a moment. "Kelly, I'm sorry you're not pregnant. It would have been awful if you were, but for a few days I started thinking I was going to be a father. I'd never thought of that before. I kind of liked it."

She nodded, handed him the fallen crutch and turned toward the kitchen, afraid to let him see her expression as she blinked back tears.

He sat at the table, accepted the coffee she gave him and watched her as she began to dry the dishes.

"Now tell me what you were talking about earlier," he said heavily.

Twelve

She poured herself a cup of coffee and joined him at the table, sitting opposite him.

"This scare gave me time to think. I'd like to have children, but not like my mother did, if I can help it. I want my child or children to grow up surrounded by love and with a feeling of belonging. If I'd been pregnant, I would have cared for and loved the baby more than anything. But I would always worry about what would happen if I died young, like my mother did."

"You wouldn't have had it alone."

She looked up at that, surprised. Then shrugged. "Doesn't matter now, we're not having a baby."

He winced and took a deep gulp of the scalding coffee.

"But it proved to me that I would like to establish roots. I'd like to get married, start a family and be a part of the community. San Francisco was too big for me, but Taylorville would be perfect."

"Time enough for all that," he said, a feeling of panic starting.

"Sure. But I don't need to waste the time now. I think Althea knows she's not in the running anymore. Our charade can end. Then I can start dating other men. Maybe find someone who wants to marry me."

"So much for love," he said harshly, glaring at her. Panic threatened to choke him. It was too soon. He wasn't ready to let her go, though he knew he'd have to eventually.

"What?"

"Didn't you say you loved me?" His eyes held hers.

She nodded, then broke their gaze, looking at her coffee. No sense in letting him see the lie in her eyes. "Yes, but I can get over that. And I would make someone a good wife and a good mother to his children. Love would surely come." Her heart pounded so loudly she was sure he must hear it. The words were so forced she knew he'd call her on the lie.

"Dammit, I don't want you with another man!" Kit growled.

"You don't want me, but you don't want anyone else to have me, either? That hardly seems fair to me," she said reasonably.

His hand caught hers across the table. Slowly he tightened his grip and pulled, forcing her out of her seat, around the end of the table.

"Come here and I'll show you how much I want you," he said, his voice low and hard.

"Not that way." She was mesmerized by his eyes. His hand was tight around hers, but not painful. The grip sent pulses of awareness through her. She stumbled around the table's edge and came up to him. He pushed back his chair and pulled her down onto his lap, his hand releasing her to encircle her, pulling her hard against him and lowering his mouth to find hers.

Kelly gave herself up to the delight of his embrace, wondering how he could ever think she'd even look at another man, loving him as much as she did. Had he been blinded in that accident, as well?

She opened her mouth and let her tongue skim the softness of his lips, seeking admittance, finding him and mating with his tongue as the dizzy spirals of passion built.

His hand roamed over her back, pulling her tightly against him, tracing the indentation by her spine. He eased her back slightly and one hand slipped under her shirt, moving easily against her heated skin.

"You're so soft," he whispered, his lips moving against her mouth, then nibbling on her cheeks, her jaw, the tender skin of her throat.

When he found her unbound breasts, he cupped first one then the other, squeezing gently, teasing the nipples into hard peaks. "No bra?" he asked as his hand fondled her, caressed her, drove her to distraction.

Eagerly her mouth found his again. She shook her head, wanting to tell him she had not been expecting visitors, but unable to stop kissing him long enough to find her voice.

Heat invaded every cell in her body, and the deep pull of desire began to build. One arm encircled his neck, her other hand wandered over the strong muscles defined beneath his shirt. Opening one button, then another, she slipped her hand in to find the warm strength of his chest, and drag her nails over his skin, reveling in his reaction.

Kit's hand left her breast and moved over her ribs, then lower to her belly, unsnapping her jeans, easing down the zipper. She stilled, but he was only rubbing her belly, his hand warm and comforting.

"Does your tummy hurt with your period?" he asked, rubbing her gently, his fingers brushing the top of her bikini panties, but not venturing lower.

She shook her head, snuggling against his neck, her breathing still ragged and heavy. He soothed her and petted her and she forgot what they'd been talking about. She forgot about everything but the way his body felt against hers, how his hand alternately soothed and inflamed her. And how much she loved him.

"It's going to be a long few days," he said, kissing her forehead.

She nodded, lassitude spreading throughout her body from his soothing touch. She took a deep breath, immediately excited by the heady scent of him, his own spicy aftershave, his body heat, the scent of love in the air. Her fingers pressed against his chest, feeling his tight nipple, the pulse of his heart and the heat rising from his skin.

Time drifted by as Kelly floated on a sea of contentment and peace. It was so right to be with Kit like this. She loved him so much and knew he must love her. If she could only get him to admit it.

Minutes, hours, days later he stirred, kissing her on her temple. "We've got to stop this or I'm going to forget you're having your period," he said at last.

Kelly nodded, not moving.

"I have to go to Stockton to get a birthday present for Sally. Come with me," he said.

"Okay." She probably should have hesitated, shown some sign of reluctance, but she couldn't. She'd take whatever time she could get with him.

He sat her up and pulled up her zipper, fastening her snap and straightening her top. Kelly kept one arm around his neck, the other hand inside his shirt, watching him with love-filled eyes. With a sigh she pulled back and calmly buttoned his shirt.

"What are we getting Sally in Stockton?"

"I don't know. Any ideas?"

They discussed various presents Kit could get his sister-in-law as they drove into the large valley town. He headed to the enclosed mall on the north side of town. Pulling into a parking slot, he turned off the engine and glanced at Kelly, taking her hand and toying with it a moment.

"If you hold this out to help me, I won't bite it off," he said whimsically. "I brought the wheelchair today. I don't like to use the crutches on the slick floors in the mall."

She tightened her fingers around his and smiled, but said nothing, afraid to say the wrong thing.

"I need your help. Can you get the chair out of the back and bring it to my door?"

"Sure." She leaned over and kissed him lightly on the mouth. "Was that so hard?" she asked gently.

"Maybe not from you, but I don't want any of the ranch hands kissing me," he said.

She burst out laughing and climbed down from the high cab. In only moments they were on their way into the mall.

"You never said when Sally's birthday is. I want to get her something, too," Kelly said as she walked along beside him.

"It's not too soon. I wanted to get the gift in plenty of time."

She glanced down at him, curious at his odd tone. His hat hid his face.

"Like how soon?"

He looked up to meet her eyes. "A couple of months."

"It's a couple of months away and we had to come out today?"

"I figured I'd need an excuse to get you to come with me today. So I used that."

She was touched. Didn't he know yet that she'd go with him just for the asking? Rubbing his shoulder lightly, she wished they could hold hands as they moved along, but he needed both hands to propel the chair. "I would have come if you'd just asked."

"Not if you were busy getting Beth to set you up with her cousin," he growled, frowning as he looked away.

She smiled secretly and prudently said nothing.

They enjoyed themselves, spending endless hours examining everything from clothes to jewelry to shoes to knickknacks. Kit finally settled on a camera. Kelly found a pretty scarf she thought Sally would like.

They ate at one of the restaurants in the mall and then wandered around eating chocolate chip cookies, just window-shopping and spending time together.

"My feet hurt," Kelly said late in the afternoon. She was ready to leave. They'd been in almost every shop in the entire complex. Kit was carrying the purchases they'd made and she was tired of all the shopping.

"I thought women shopped till they dropped."

"Well, I'm dropping. Let's go home now."

"Fine. Want a ride?" He patted his thighs.

She nodded, settling herself crossways on his lap and smiling gleefully. He pushed them forward and they headed for the door nearest the truck.

"This is fun," she said, glancing around at the other shoppers who had stopped to stare at them. Giggling a little, she ducked her head.

"I think people are looking at us."

"Probably wishing they could ride," he said in amusement.

"The women probably wish they could be me, sitting on your lap, but not just for the ride," she said, noting the expression on some faces as they scooted by.

"Do you kiss and drive at the same time?" she asked audaciously, kissing his cheek.

He stopped the chair. "No, but I can do one at a time." He caught her face in his hands and brought his lips down on hers in a hard kiss.

She was flustered and laughing when he released her. "Not here."

He laughed and started the chair again. "You brought it on, Miss Smarty. Remember who you're dealing with."

"Sure, Mr. Macho Rodeo Cowboy," she murmured, knowing now how reckless and wild he must have been when he was younger. No wonder his reputation was intact. He'd not changed all that much.

Kit took her hand as he drove toward home, threading his fingers through it and resting it on his hard thigh. Kelly felt a warm contentment spread through her and her mood was almost euphoric.

"Want to stay for dinner? I can fix some linguine."

"What's that? Yuppified city food?"

"Yep. Too bad I can't make sushi."

He made a face. "What's wrong with beef?"

She laughed. "You'll like linguine."

"I'll try anything once. I like living on the edge of danger."

"Hardly the edge of danger."

"Being with you is dangerous enough," he muttered.

"Why?"

"You start a man to thinking things he had no business thinking," he said.

"Like?"

"Like nothing. Tell me how you make linguine."

Recognizing the stubborn tilt to his jaw, she complied. Kit helped with dinner, which surprised Kelly.

"I didn't know you were so domestic," she said as they worked companionably in the kitchen. He'd made the garlic bread while she was making the tomato sauce and pasta, and had cleaned and cut the vegetables for their salad.

"And that surprises you? I'm a bachelor. How do you think I would eat if I couldn't fix some things? I'm real good at steak and baked potatoes."

"I bet. But Sally does that at the ranch."

"Now. But I lived a lot of years alone before she and Clint moved in. And I needed their help when I was first home from the hospital. I don't so much now."

She was thoughtful. Was their arrangement now just habit? "Do they want a house of their own?"

He looked up at her, an arrested expression on his face. "I don't know. They've never said anything." He went back to the salad. "Though I'm sure they will when they start having kids. My house isn't all that big. We've turned the third bedroom into an office. I'll have to ask them."

"Could you manage on your own?"

"If I had someone in to clean every so often I could. Tell me some more about your life in the big bad city."

Picking up on his desire to change the subject, Kelly began describing her friends, the routine she'd enjoyed the past few years. From that the conversation drifted to music, books and other friends.

They moved to the sofa in the living room, neglecting to turn on the lights. As Kelly lay snuggled against him, she knew she'd never find a better man to care for her. For her to love.

"Kit." This would shatter their evening.

"Umm?" They had been silent for a few moments, he toying with the fingers of one of her hands.

"Tell me more about the operation," she said softly, holding her breath against his reaction.

He sighed, dropping her hand, pulling his arm from around her shoulders.

"There's nothing to talk about."

"Yes, there is. Tell me." She clutched his arm, refusing to allow him to move away. She knew he wanted to.

"I told you before it's not your business."

"Tell me about the operation," she insisted.

He sighed and turned away. "Dammit. It's some experimental operation at Stanford that is supposed to improve muscle response from damaged nerves. The operation itself would only take a couple of hours. But the convalescence and physical therapy would take weeks, months."

"And it would be painful?"

"Probably. God, Kelly, you don't know what it was like before. Even when I was asleep I could feel the pain. It wasn't just an ache like falling off a horse, or being stepped on by a steer. It was cutting and sharp and endless." He rubbed his face with both hands, dropped them to his thighs.

"I know I don't know what it was like. It must have been awful. Didn't the medicine help?"

"I didn't want painkillers. I was taking no chances of becoming addicted."

She blinked. "Kit, they wouldn't let you become addicted. You can use the medicine to control the worst of the pain. Would the operation allow you to walk better? Maybe ride better?"

"Hell, who knows if it would do anything. I said it was experimental. Sometimes it helps." He hadn't thought about it since Althea had so cruelly rejected him in the hospital. He wondered now if he should have. With more mobility he'd be able to do more. Offer more. To someone like Kelly. To Kelly. Would it make enough of a difference to change things? Allow him to become more of the kind of man she should have?

"Would it make anything worse?" she asked softly.

"There's a certain risk." But wouldn't it be worth it for her? If it was unsuccessful, he'd be no worse off than he was right now. And if it worked, maybe he'd have something worth offering to her.

She knelt beside him on the sofa, taking his head in both her hands, her palms caressing the strong, stubborn line of his jaw as she turned him to face her in the dim light.

"Kit, if you decide on the operation, I'll be there with you every day, sassy mouth and all. You won't be alone. I'll fix it so I sleep in your room, even. I would be with you every moment, and if the pain gets bad, we'll make love and you'll forget it."

He stared at her, a lopsided smile starting at her idea for suppressing pain. Then his eyes darkened. "There's a chance I could walk better, be more mobile."

"Darling, if you could be more mobile, it would be wonderful for you."

"For you, maybe," he muttered, his hands taking hers from his face. Would she settle for that? Could he offer her a life as his wife if he was more mobile?

"No, dammit, for you. I've told you before I love you just as you are and if you never walked across the room again I wouldn't care. But for you, to be as free as you can be, it's important. If you'd been a businessman stuck behind a desk every day, it wouldn't matter as much. But your life is out there." She swept her hand toward the window. "You can ride now. Wouldn't it be grand to walk across your fields, as well?"

He refused to answer. He wanted it so badly he could taste it. Feared losing her so badly he could hardly breathe. It was such a risk. Could he do it? Gathering his crutches, he left without even telling her goodbye, the possibilities pounding in his brain.

Kelly's eyes filled with tears and she remained seated on the sofa, listening to his truck drive off. She loved him so much, and he had never said he loved her. She knew he wanted her, he desired her. He couldn't keep his hands off her when they were together. But he'd never said he loved her. Was she a fool to continue to kid herself? If he cared for her as she did for him, surely by this time he would have said something.

The next morning Kelly woke late. She'd had a restless night, finding trouble sleeping. When she did sleep, her dreams were filled with longing for Kit. Every time he turned from her and walked away. Listlessly she rose and dressed. Wandering down the stairs, she looked around her house. She'd been happy here, but she couldn't stay forever loving a man who couldn't love her back.

Two days later she'd made up her mind. She'd go back to the city for a time. Try to decide what to do with her life. If she had to, she could sell Aunt Margaret's house, buy another one in some other small town. Or move back to San Francisco for good. She smiled wistfully. She liked small towns. She still longed to belong somewhere. Maybe the next stop would be her last.

Kelly called Judith and begged the use of her guest room for a couple of weeks. With a place to stay assured, she began to pack. The new story was mapped out. She could work on it in San Francisco. Once she decided what she was going to do with her future, she'd have to come back. Either to stay, or to sell the house. But she'd worry about that later. First she had to say goodbye.

That afternoon she drove out to the Lockford ranch. She wanted one last look at Sam. That was something else she'd have to take care of. She'd ask Beth if she could board him at her dad's until Kelly decided what she'd do.

Kit was working on his truck when Kelly drove into the yard, the hood propped open, his virile body leaning against the fender. He turned and watched as she drove up beside him. Kelly hesitated a moment when she saw him. Ignoring her own jangling nerves, she got out of her car and walked up to him.

"Hello."

"Hello yourself, darlin'."

His eyes were hooded, watchful, but he met her more than halfway, reaching out to kiss her, his tongue flicking out to touch her lips before she pulled back.

"Came to see Sam?" Kit asked easily. Leaning casually against the truck, his crutches almost forgotten, he looked heart-stoppingly sexy.

Kelly took a deep breath. "Yes. Actually, to say goodbye for a while." She looked around the yard, over toward the corral, afraid to meet his gaze.

"Goodbye?"

"I'm going to the city for a couple of weeks." She bit her lip and faced him bravely. "I'm going to ask Beth if her dad would board Sam until I decide what I'm going to do."

"What the hell do you mean, until you decide what to do? What are you talking about? How long are you going to the city for?" His voice had a hard edge to it.

"Long enough to decide what I'm going to do with my life," she said firmly.

"What's wrong with your life the way it is?" he growled. God, she was talking about leaving? He wanted to pull her into his arms and never let her go.

"I can't keep on this way," she murmured, her eyes sad.

"So you're running back to the city?"

"Well, for a couple of weeks, anyway. Then I'll decide where I'll live. Maybe I'll sell Aunt Margaret's house and find something in another town. Maybe I'll stay in the city. I don't know just yet."

"Kelly..."

She shook her head. "Once you told me I'd get a truck-load of heartache if I set my sights on you. Well, you were right. I'm not such a masochist to stay where I'm not wanted."

"I want you!"

"Sure, to warm your bed. It's not enough!" Anger and frustration echoed in her voice.

Instantly he recalled their morning conversation of a few days ago. *She would start looking for a husband. Someone to settle down with and raise a family.* Suddenly he was afraid. God, how would he stand seeing her with another man, know that man was sleeping with her, loving her, and she was loving him back? He couldn't bear it! It would be bad enough if she went back to San Francisco and he never saw her again. But if she settled nearby, he'd see her over the years with somebody else. It would tear him apart! The fear grew until it was bigger than what he felt when he rode the bulls, bigger than what he'd felt when the doctors had told him he wouldn't walk again. She was his and he couldn't let her go, no matter what!

But how could he tie her to a cripple? How could he offer her life with a partial man? She deserved so much more! Yet he couldn't bear the thought of losing her to another man. God, he'd lost so much—the life he'd always thought he would have, the freedom of going where he wanted, doing what he wanted. Even losing Althea didn't compare to what he'd feel if he lost Kelly.

Staring at her, he also remembered her words that night in the truck. She had said it wouldn't matter if her husband couldn't walk or hear or see if he loved her and she loved him. Did she mean it? Dare he count on that? Because he suddenly knew beyond all doubt that he couldn't let her go. If she truly loved him, then she was his, because he just could not let her go.

She studied him silently for a long moment, then gave a sad smile. Nodding at him, she stepped past and walked toward the barn.

Kit watched her walk away. He would not let her go. Dammit, it wasn't what she deserved, but he loved her and he was damn well going to keep her in Taylorville. If she couldn't cope with his handicap, she'd have one last chance to say so. Impatiently he watched her stroke the pony's head.

Just as he was about to storm over and demand she stay, Sally joined her, excited with news.

Kelly listened, intrigued. Twice she glanced over to Kit. The hood of the truck was still up, but he was not working, his attention focused on them. Kelly met his eyes across the distance as she listened to Sally. Then she smiled and started walking toward Kit.

"Well?" he said when she reached him, wondering uneasily what Sally had told her. Wondering how he could bind her to him so tightly she'd never even think of getting away. How could he ever have thought he could let her go?

"I hear Clint and Sally are going to be building their own place."

"Yep. Time they had a place of their own." His eyes were hungry for her.

"Mmm-hmm." She glanced toward Sally, then back to him. "I also heard Althea returned to Stockton."

"That's right."

"Several weeks ago," she clarified.

He nodded.

"Right after the dance?"

He nodded again, his gaze steady. Tension pulsed in the air.

"Then what's all this charade been about?"

He reached out and threaded his fingers through hers, tracing soft patterns on the back of her hand, panic threatening. His heart was pounding, the blood rushing through his veins so hard he could hardly hear her. He couldn't let her go. But would she really stay?

"You and me," he murmured, his eyes meeting hers.

Kelly was having a hard time concentrating, shivering at the sensations rippling through her at Kit's touch. Her breasts filled and ached in longing. The tiny fire at the pit of her being ignited and glowed. How could she ever stop loving him?

"Why didn't you tell me she'd left?"

"It wasn't important."

"I thought she was the reason for the charade."

"There's no charade, Kelly. Maybe there was for one night, but not since then."

Her heart began pounding as she allowed herself to be caught up in his heated gaze. Permitted a tiny glimmer of hope to bloom.

"Then what have we had?"

"A courtship. Rough, erratic and not very romantic, maybe."

She smiled. "No maybe about it, buster."

"But a courtship?"

She nodded slowly, hope daring to grow.

His hand drew her closer, until she touched him, breast to chest, thigh to thigh. "You belong here."

She felt a warm glow expand through her body. "I want to belong somewhere," she said wistfully.

"You belong here, with me. To me."

He pulled her firmly into his arms, anchoring her against him.

"Since when?" she asked lazily, a small secret smile teasing her lips, her heart racing in sudden delight.

"I'm not sure since when. But at least since that first time in my bed. You sure as hell aren't going looking for another man. I'm man enough for you and always will be." His lips blazed a hot trail against her neck.

"Since when, cowboy?" Hope flared as she pulled back to gaze into his determined face. *Please love me.*

"Since the beginning of time, darlin'. And if you have any doubts, let's adjourn to my bedroom and I'll prove it to you again."

She giggled softly and kissed his jaw. "Sally's standing not fifty feet away and you think we can just up and hop in your bed?"

"Only if you have any doubts about what I'm saying."

"And that is?"

"You belong to me, Kelly. I can't stand the thought of you with any other man. It won't be a great bargain—"

"Shh. It will be the best bargain of my life. I love you, Kit."

"I love you, Kelly, darlin'." His lips claimed hers in a searing kiss. He had to have her. She was fire in his blood.

With her he was whole again. He'd do everything in his power to make her happy. He'd never let her go.

"Hey, you two, what's going on over there?" Sally's loud question interrupted.

"We're celebrating an engagement," Kit said firmly, his eyes looking deep into Kelly's. She nodded happily and leaned forward for another kiss.

She knew she was shining with happiness, and when she looked at Kit she had to laugh. He looked as arrogant and proud as if he'd invented the institution of marriage.

"And at our wedding, you can dance with me," Kelly murmured as she floated in her unexpected happiness. She had come to say goodbye, and now would stay forever.

"Kelly, that's something I can't do," Kit protested, frustrated by her damned optimism, yet knowing he wouldn't change a single thing about her.

"Want to bet?" she asked.

He gazed at her for a long moment, seeing the love and determination in her eyes, and his heart melted. He loved her so much! The anguish of the past was forgotten as he faced a bright future with the woman he finally had allowed himself to love.

"I'll think about it," he said, sweeping her against him for a hard kiss.

Epilogue

Eight months later...

Slowly he lifted the veil from her face and gazed down at her, love shining in her sparkling blue eyes. Her lips lifted in a saucy smile and she parted them as if to speak.

"No," his voice was hushed, only she could hear. "I've waited a long time for this moment, don't say one sassy thing to spoil it. I love you." He claimed her lips with his, his hands warm and loving on her shoulders. Almost bursting with pride, he turned her to face the congregation as the minister introduced them as man and wife.

Kit offered his arm, took the cane from his brother and together he and his new wife started slowly down the aisle.

Kelly beamed with happiness, her hand tightening on her husband's arm. She glanced at her new mother-in-law already feeling like she belonged forever to the wonderful family that had welcomed her so warmly all those months ago. Nodded to Beth and Michael. Winked at Molly Benson's teary smile. Smiled happily at Jefferies knowing look.

As Clint and Judith fell in behind them Kelly raised her eyes to Kit's. "I wouldn't have spoiled it," she said softly, grinning audaciously. "This is wonderful for me, too, you know."

"I never can tell with you," he muttered, thankful the ceremony had gone off without a hitch. One more task and he'd be free to hustle his bride away from the crowd and have her to himself.

In only a few moments they were at the grange hall where the Lockfords had arranged the reception. The entire town had been invited. Kelly had invited her friends from the city and the place was full. The band was playing, the food was sumptuous and their happiness contagious.

"Never thought I'd see the day," Jefferies said as he came up to congratulate them. "Sure glad I was there at the beginning."

"Which was almost the end. If he'd run over me I wouldn't be here today," Kelly said, her mocking grin teasing her new husband.

The music started. A waltz.

"Mrs. Lockford, if I may have the pleasure?" Kit reached out his hand and took hers. She smiled as she moved in to dance with him. He handed the cane to Jefferies. "I'll just lean on you for balance," he said softly as he gathered his soft pretty wife into his arms.

"Satisfied?" he asked as they moved slowly around the floor. Other couples gradually joined in.

Kelly looked up and nodded, her eyes full of love. "But it wasn't for me, you know," she said, her arms hugging him tightly for a second. "It was always for you. I fell in love with an irate cowboy who didn't like being called an idiot for driving like a maniac. But I didn't care if he could walk or not."

"It wasn't as bad as I thought," he admitted, thinking briefly over the last few months, the operation, the stay at the hospital. Kelly had been with him every step. The convalescence and physical therapy had gone better than even his doctor had anticipated. All because of her.

"Because I was there," she said bragging.

He chuckled and let his left hand drift down to her hip, moving it swiftly back up when he realized where they were. "Probably. Though we never did try your proven method for getting over pain."

"It wasn't as bad as you led me to believe, though I'm so happy it was successful. Walking with a cane isn't so bad, is it? And if you follow the exercise program, one day you can give that up."

"I'll always limp, but then I'll be almost as good as new. But you are one pushy woman."

"And you are one stubborn cowboy." She was silent for a few moments, enjoying the special treat of dancing at her wedding with her husband. The music was dreamy, the day was perfect and a happy, fulfilling life stretched out endlessly before them.

"I have one other request," she said softly.

"No."

"You haven't even heard it yet," she protested in mock disapproval.

"Doesn't matter. I can't do any more."

She smiled smugly. "You can do this!" Her eyes were dancing. "I want a baby."

He hesitated, then rested his cheek against hers. It would make their life together perfect to have a house full of sassy girls and rough-and-ready boys. Kelly had brought him more than he'd ever expected to have. She would never stop filling his heart with love.

"I'll think about it," he said, already anxious to leave the reception and make her his wife forever.

* * * * *

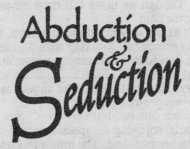
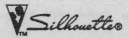

MILLION DOLLAR SWEEPSTAKES (III)

Silhouette celebrates motherhood in May with...

Debbie Macomber
Jill Marie Landis
Gina Ferris Wilkins

in

Three Mothers & a Cradle

Join three award-winning authors in this
beautiful collection you'll treasure forever.
The same antique, hand-crafted cradle
connects these three heartwarming romances,
which celebrate the joys and excitement of
motherhood. Makes the perfect gift for yourself
or a loved one!

A special celebration of love,

Only from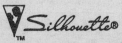

—where passion lives.

A new series from Nancy Martin

Who says opposites don't attract?

Three sexy bachelors
should've seen trouble coming
when each meets a woman
who makes his blood boil—
and not just because she's beautiful....

In March—
THE PAUPER AND THE PREGNANT PRINCESS (#916)

In May—
THE COP AND THE CHORUS GIRL (#927)

In September—
THE COWBOY AND THE CALENDAR GIRL

Watch the sparks fly as these handsome hunks fall for
the women they swore they didn't want!
Only from Silhouette Desire.